BURIED SECRETS

Kevin O'Hagan

Grosvenor House
Publishing Limited

This book is published by
Grosvenor House Publishing Ltd
Link House
140 The Broadway, Tolworth, Surrey, KT6 7HT.
www.grosvenorhousepublishing.co.uk

A CIP record for this book
is available from the British Library

ISBN 978-1-80381-734-7

For my wonderful grandchildren.
May you live your dreams.

Acknowledgements

As always, my huge thanks to the 'Usual Suspects', who helped me on my journey from getting this story from an idea to print.

My daughter Lauren for the proofreading, grammar and spellcheck.

My son Tom for another excellent cover design.

My publishers for all their help and guidance, especially Melanie Bartle.

My wife Tina for her continued support of my writing and the tea and coffee.

Author's Note

Some cities, towns and locations in this novel exist in real life; others are purely fictional, as may be their geographical placings. Landscapes, names and layouts take on another imaginary status in this book. The legend and myth surrounding the story *Buried Secrets* is just that. All the characters are purely fictional, as are their stories. Thank you for indulging me to help in creating this story.

Side note: St. Columba did exist in history, but some of his story takes on a fictional life for this book. What is fact or fiction is up to you to decide.

A Word from the Author

I had no immediate plans to bring the character of Joe Regan back, but when I had an idea come floating into my head about buried Celtic treasures, ruined abbeys and the Emerald Isle, it all seemed to fit the profile of Joe.

Ex-cop, antiques dealer, bit of a history buff and of Irish heritage. Yes, the time seemed right to reintroduce Joe Regan and his girlfriend Maggie Scott, place them in Ireland and let them yet again get embroiled in a good murder mystery.

Now don't panic, readers. We haven't drifted into the territory of *Heartbeat* or *Midsomer Murders*.

Against the backdrop of beautiful countryside, legends and history is a gritty plot with its usual twists and turns.

Danger and unease are never far away.

Nobody can be trusted or seems as they are.

The beauty of being in charge of your own story and characters is that you can do what you want with them as long as it doesn't stray too far from their personality. I enjoyed introducing a myriad of different characters here, all with their own strengths and weaknesses.

I had a lot of fun writing this book and giving Joe Regan another run out.

I hope you enjoy it.

If you haven't met Joe before, you may wish to also read his first adventure in *Killing Time*.

Kevin O'Hagan, September 2023

Prologue

Declan Byrne woke with a start. He had not realised that he had nodded off. He glanced at the clock on the mantlepiece. 2.00am. It was late. He had been so absorbed in his research and studies that he had lost all track of time. But something had awoken him.

A noise?

Yes, he thought that he'd heard something.

Declan was alone in the house, except for his golden labrador, Oscar, who was sleeping on the rug in front of the dying embers of a welcoming fire in the ornate fireplace.

Declan listened again, but all was quiet. The only sounds were the ticking of the clock, the faint stirring of the wind outside and the distant lapping of the sea.

Maybe I imagined it?

He was sat at his desk in the study, his favourite room in the house. It was his bolthole and sanctuary. The room was filled with antiques and interesting historical artefacts. Awards and scholarly certificates of achievement adorned the walls, along with bookcases crammed with scholarly reading. A lifetime's work and passion.

Declan Byrne was a retired professor of Irish history who had worked at the prestigious Trinity College in Dublin for over 25 years. The university was world renowned and Ireland's oldest surviving one. It had produced the innovative minds of people such as Oscar Wilde and Samuel Beckett, amongst many more.

Declan had loved his job. It wasn't just the teaching of a subject that he was absolutely passionate about since he was a young man; it was also his unlimited access to the university's famous library, which housed such works of art as the *Book of Keels*. The ninth-century illuminated manuscript contained the four gospels of the New Testament. It was a true cultural treasure of Ireland.

As a historian, Declan loved being around such literary masterpieces. Celtic history was his obsession. He was viewed as the last word on the subject in some quarters.

These days, he worked as a part-time consultant to the library and still did the very occasional lecture or workshop. His knowledge of Irish history was second to none and after many years of retirement, he was still highly regarded and sought after.

In recent times through his own research, he had stumbled upon something which was truly amazing. The possibility of an ancient legend being true and treasures untold. All the evidence he had accumulated over the years pointed in that direction. He was incredibly excited by this discovery; hence, his exhaustive research and the many late nights.

Declan knew that he should go to bed, but his mind was buzzing. Sleep would not be forthcoming if he did.

He removed his reading glasses and placed them on his desk. He briefly regarded his mobile phone, but there were no messages. Occasionally, a student from America would drop him an email forgetting the time difference in the countries.

He rubbed his tired eyes and glanced at the framed photograph by the reading lamp. The photograph was of his late wife, Mary. He had lost her to cancer five years ago. Not a day went by when he did not think about her and miss her dearly.

They had found each other later in life and had been married for 20 years. They had lived a happy and enriched life right up until Mary's breast cancer diagnosis. The cancer was aggressive and finally spread into her bones. Within a year of finding this out, she had passed away.

The big house they had lived in now seemed very empty. It was a Victorian waterfront structure, which Declan and Mary had fell in love with two decades ago. It was everything they had been looking for. The house and location had been precious to them both.

After Mary's death, Declan had contemplated selling up, but had never got around to seriously doing anything about it.

Declan had come to marriage in his mid-fifties. He had been convinced that he would remain a bachelor until he met Mary Connell at a friend's birthday party. She was bright, witty, intelligent and a handsome woman. A complete catch. At that time, she had been an A&E nurse at St. James's Hospital, the biggest hospital in Dublin.

Declan could not believe that she was attracted to him. They started dating and, after six months, they got married. His one regret was that they had been too old for children.

They did manage to travel, however, which was a passion of theirs. Before Mary's diagnosis, they had fulfilled a lifetime dream of cruising the Caribbean.

This was where the photograph of Mary had been taken, on a sun-kissed beach in St. Lucia. Happy memories.

Declan was now 76 years of age. He felt that he was too old and too set in his ways for change. Besides, he loved the house which was situated in the affluent suburb and seaside town of Dalkey.

The town was steeped in history dating back to Viking times. It also held one of the world's most prestigious book festivals every year. Music to the ears of a scholar such as Declan Byrne.

The town was also known as a millionaires' row for the rich and famous. Such names as Maeve Binchy, the author, and George Bernard Shaw, the playwright, both made Dalkey their home at one time or another. So too had Hollywood film actors Pierce Brosnan and Mel Gibson, as well as musicians Bono, Enya and Van Morrison.

The famous house, Ischia, located on the illustrious Sorrento Road had even been home to Matt Damon for a portion of the COVID-19 lockdown when the US actor was in Ireland filming *The Last Duel*. The house overlooked the Irish Sea, standing at a palatial 5,500 square feet.

Dalkey truly was a magical place. Declan could not see himself living anywhere else.

He decided to make himself a mug of hot chocolate and then continue his work. There was nobody to share his bed with these days. Nobody to answer to. His time was his own.

Declan had got used to his own company. Twice a week, Mrs Fergus, the housekeeper, came to clean the place and do the chores. This kept the big old house ticking over. She also liked to bring in the occasional apple pie or steak and kidney pudding, which Declan loved. Most of the time, his own cooking involved a microwave. A scholar he was, a cook never.

Apart from Mrs Fergus, he did not see many people. Since Mary's passing, he had become more and more reclusive. Plus, many health issues prevented him from getting out as much as he would like. The house had become his sanctuary.

One old friend that he did keep in contact with was Dermot Leary who had been a librarian at Trinity. They had shared many a cup of tea or a glass of Jameson's over a good chat when both were working at the university.

Both men loved their books and history. They also shared a keen interest in antiques. They were kindred spirits in a way.

Back in his younger days, Dermot had been in the forces. He did not talk much about it. It seemed to be a period that he would rather forget. But Declan did believe that his old friend may have made officer status.

On leaving the army, he went on to further his education and obtained a bachelor's degree, which led to his job at Trinity.

He had recently retired from university life and lived in central Dublin just off the famous Grafton Street. He now owned a gift shop selling all things Irish with a Taiwan stamp on the bottom to the millions of tourists who flocked there. They did not seem to mind. One coffee mug or drinking glass with an image of Oscar Wilde on it pretty much looked like another.

Dermot was not the type of man ready for pipe and slippers just yet. Although he was 68, he still ran three miles each morning.

Once a month, Dermot would visit Declan's home. They would still talk enthusiastically about their time at Trinity and Celtic history into the small hours.

Their main area of interest was the life and times of St. Columba. This man had led an incredibly interesting life. Much was still not known about him. Also, it was difficult to separate fact from legend.

Dermot had visited Declan in his home the previous weekend, and Declan had been excited to share his recent discoveries about St. Columba with him, although he had sworn his old friend to complete secrecy until further notice.

Dermot was honoured to be privy to Declan's discovery. If proved right, it would be worldwide news and propel Declan Byrne to even greater fame and fortune.

Some men seemed destined to find greatness, while others saw it pass them by no matter how hard they tried.

Declan put the journal in which he had been writing into the top left-hand drawer of his desk. He then removed a thin silver chain from his neck, which had a key on the end, and used it to lock the drawer. He returned the chain to his neck.

He reached for his cane, walked to the study door and opened it. He immediately knew that something was not right.

He felt a draught coming from somewhere as if a window had been left open.

Declan then realised that he had been so immersed in his work since early evening that he had forgotten to put the burglar alarm on.

He walked slowly into the large hallway. His left hip was particularly painful tonight. The operation to replace it was still a few months away.

Damn getting old.

His mind was still razor sharp. It was just his body that was failing him.

He now looked over by the front door to see the alarm pad on the wall. As he suspected, the alarm was unarmed.

Declan felt the draught again. It seemed to be coming from the drawing room to his right.

Walking through the open door into the room, he switched on the light and saw the curtains on the window blowing in the wind.

Declan paced across the room and that was when he saw the broken glass on the carpet.

He pulled back the curtain to reveal an open window.

A sudden feeling of dread filled his being.

This must have been the noise I thought I heard earlier. Had someone broken in?

He turned around quickly, nearly losing his balance. His eyes surveyed the room.

Nothing moved.

Everything seemed in place.

He wished he had brought Oscar with him. That said, the soppy old thing would probably lick a would-be burglar to death.

Moving as quickly as he was able, he headed out into the hallway switching lights on as he went.

The snug and kitchen were empty. All seemed as it should.

Declan contemplated taking a knife from the wooden block on the kitchen worktop, but decided that maybe he was overreacting. Plus, who did he think he was? Rambo?

Moving back to the hallway, he glanced up the staircase into the pockets of shadow that lurked there. As a young boy, he had hated going up the stairs at night on his own and would try and wait for his older sister to go to bed so she could accompany him. That was not going to happen now as she had lived in Australia for 20 odd years.

He swallowed hard and slowly walked to the foot of the stairs.

There were four bedrooms and a bathroom up there.

A lot of choices for someone to hide in.

He then thought that he heard the creak of a floorboard overhead.

A footstep?

Panic swept over him.

What was he going to do if he confronted a burglar anyway?

Declan headed back to his study where his mobile phone sat on his desk. He was going to phone the police. Better to be safe than sorry. He was no hero.

Because of its wealth and 'home to the stars' reputation, Dalkey had been the target of burglars on more than one occasion.

Declan's house contained many antiques of value that he cherished. That said, he was not going to tangle with a burglar over them. He was handsomely insured.

He moved into his study and immediately saw that Oscar was not by the fireside. To his dread, he also saw that the French doors were ajar.

They had been locked.

Earlier that evening, Declan had opened them and stood in the garden enjoying the one cigar of the day that he allowed himself. Mary never liked him smoking indoors and he still abided by his late wife's wishes.

It was a ritual, weather permitting. He always used the engraved gold lighter that Mary had given him to light that luxurious Havana. It was a present for his last birthday when she was alive.

Suddenly, Declan remembered that as he was coming back into his study that evening after smoking, his phone had rung. He could not swear that he had turned the key in the lock, as he did most evenings.

The phone call had been from an old student of his, Thomas Cahill, who was overseeing an archaeological dig at the remains of a Celtic abbey near Ballykin, where it is said that St. Columba had lived and worked and from where he had made his famous journey to Scotland to spread the word of Christianity.

Legend says that when he died, he was brought back to the abbey to rest – or at least some of him –along with many precious artefacts, but neither a body nor any treasures had ever been found.

Declan had been working with Thomas as an unpaid consultant and had been researching the site for any inside information which would help the dig be a success.

The abbey was the spot where Declan believed secrets buried for centuries lay ready to be discovered. Secrets which, over time, had become fabled legends with no real facts behind them. That was all about to change dramatically if Declan was right.

Thomas and his partner, Shannon Brady, were his people on the ground. He could no longer dig himself, but they could. If they dug in the right places with his guidance, there was a promise of untold wealth and fame.

He and Thomas had spoken for ten minutes or so and then Declan had gone to make a cup of coffee.

Did I forget to lock the patio door?

As his brain attempted to process this information, he sensed a movement behind him and then felt a gloved hand clamp tightly over his nose and mouth, pulling him backwards.

Declan dropped his cane.

He reached up and attempted to claw the hand away, but it gripped him like a vice.

Declan could feel his head grow light through lack of oxygen. He suffered from high blood pressure, which did not help the predicament he found himself in.

Panicking, he again tried to remove the hand, but it was hopeless. The person was far too strong for Declan.

As Declan's struggling became redundant, he saw a man enter through the patio door. He wore a balaclava and held a knife in his hand. The blade was covered in what looked like blood.

The man went to Declan's desk and searched the surface, rifling through the paperwork upon it. Declan saw him pocket a few things, but could not see what.

He then hissed, "Get me the key," to the person restraining Byrne.

This person reached up and ripped the chain from the professor's neck. It was there as he had been told.

The keychain was thrown to the other man who immediately used it to open the top left-hand drawer of the desk.

Declan suddenly realized what they were after.

No, not my journal. Take the paintings, the porcelain, but not my journal. How did they know it was there? How did these people know about the key? Only he and...

Unconsciousness began to take Declan over.

He glanced across at the picture of Mary on his desk. Her smiling face looked back at him and then began to blur.

Declan was not a religious man, but if there were a heaven, how he wanted now to be reunited with his wife.

He collapsed. The shock and stress of the situation had stopped his heart.

The man holding him from behind eased the dead body of Declan Byrne to the carpet.

He looked towards his companion and whispered.

"Is that it? Did you get it?"

The other man looked up and held the journal aloft.

"Yeah, I got it."

"Right, let's get out of here. I think the old fella has croaked it."

"Shit, you clown. That wasn't meant to happen."

"It was an accident. The old boy was so frail. I didn't realise."

"Well, it's too late now. Come on. Let's go."

The two figures stepped out into the garden and over the dying body of Oscar, who had been stabbed in the belly, and disappeared into the night.

The body of Declan Byrne lay still on the floor.

The great discoveries and buried secrets that he had painstakingly researched were now taken to the grave with him. Or were they?

Chapter 1

The Land Rover Discovery navigated the winding coastal roads with expertise. Every now and then, it would have to pull in tight to let other vehicles pass that were coming in the opposite direction.

To the left were the magnificent clifftop views. The sheer drops to the sea below were exhilarating and frightening at the same time.

The coastal road from Dublin to Cork was a beautiful and wild stretch of Southern Ireland. Incredible scenes of the Irish sea and then later the Atlantic would spread out as far as the eye could see on a sunny day. The waters were a deep turquoise blue. It was truly a wonderous sight to behold.

When the weather was good, the British Isles could stand shoulder to shoulder with any other country when it came to its scenery. But when the weather was bad, this rugged and barren coastline could be foreboding and, in some cases, treacherous.

Today, on this balmy late September afternoon, it was a place of tranquil beauty.

Sat behind the wheel of the Discovery was Joe Regan, antiques dealer and ex-DCI in the Metropolitan Police. Next to him in the passenger seat was his girlfriend, Maggie Scott.

They were on a road trip.

Joe Regan's roots were in Southern Ireland. His great-grandfather, Francis, and his wife had emigrated from County Cork to London, England in the wake of the potato famine of 1845.

Joe was proud of his roots. His family had all come from County Cork and it had been a long time since Joe had visited. Too long.

As a high-ranking copper, he had always been too busy to take a holiday or to do anything outside his precious job. This cost him his marriage to his then-wife, Emma.

After surviving a particularly savage and potentially fatal attack some years back by escaped prisoner and heavy-duty villain Eddie Keen, Joe's superiors persuaded him to consider retirement or spend his remaining years in the force behind a desk. Joe could not contemplate the latter. Although he had fully recovered from the attack, he reluctantly retired from policing and had a go at starting his own business in the antiques world, which he had always had a healthy interest in since he was a boy.

He had opened Lost Treasures Antiques Emporium some seven years ago. It had been tough going at first, but he stuck at it and finally turned the corner before COVID nearly derailed him. But somehow, in those dark days, Joe got by. Not least because of Maggie.

She had been a rock supporting him all the way as she also battled to keep her own business, Blooming Flowers, afloat.

They lived and worked in the quaint little village of Oakcombe in the South West of England. A picturesque and popular destination for holidaymakers and tourists. They had been a couple for roughly two years.

Maggie had met Joe when they both had got involved in what was to be known as the 'Goodwin Murders', which had happened in and around the village and quickly became front-page news.

An antique clock with a hidden secret had been brought into Joe's shop and this had triggered a series of deadly and dangerous events. Joe had been at the centre of a major criminal case and had fought for his life once more.

Thankfully, that was in the past and, up to now, Joe had resisted any temptation to fall back into his previous role as detective.

He and Maggie had built an idyllic life in Oakcombe. A life that was a million miles away from the one he had previously in London.

Joe had properly immersed himself in the antiques business and was really making a name for himself in this field. So much so that his emporium had featured in the television programme *Antiques Road Trip* on more than one occasion.

The past week here on holiday in Ireland had been magical. It had been a while since Joe had taken a long break and he had been a teenager of around 16 when he had last set foot in the country. The visit was well overdue.

They had another week ahead of them still. The holiday would end in Cork where Joe had relatives to visit.

Joe had asked Maggie if she would like to go on this adventure back to his home country and tour around seeing the sites and maybe doing a bit of buying as well. Maggie had jumped at the chance to spend some quality downtime with the man she had grown to love and find out more about his past and family.

Her previous relationship had turned out to be a marriage to a controlling and abusive husband, which she had the courage finally to walk away from. She had moved from Cornwall and relocated to Somerset. Her relationship with Joe Regan could not be further from her old one, thank God.

Joe and Maggie had started their trip by taking the ferry from Holyhead in Anglesey, North Wales to Dublin. The 2.5-hour trip had gone smoothly. They had then stayed three days in Dublin, taking in as many of the major tourist sites as their time and schedule would allow.

They visited the Guinness Storeroom to learn how the 'black stuff' was made and sampled some, of course. Then, they went to the magnificent St Patrick's and Christchurch Cathedrals with their stunning architecture.

Next up was Trinity College and a viewing of the iconic *Book of Kells*. As an antiques dealer and appreciative of history, Joe knew that an object like this was virtually priceless, and he had been humbled to see such a wonderful book in all its splendour.

The EPIC Irish Emigration Museum gave Joe a fascinating insight into his Irish heritage and the legendary Temple Bar gave him a chance to sample some of Ireland's finest whiskeys. The headache he experienced the following morning was a testament to how good they were.

Maggie loved the shops on Grafton Street and all the colour and hubbub that went with this vibrant area, especially the street entertainers.

They even managed to fit in a photograph by the famous statue of the late rockstar, Phil Lynott, outside the Bruxelles Rock Pub on Harry Street. Dublin's favourite son and the legendary frontman of Thin Lizzy was always a popular site to visit.

Their final day in Dublin consisted of a boat trip down the river Liffey and a walk in the picturesque Phoenix Park which housed Dublin Zoo.

From there, they drove on through County Wicklow with its famous mountains sweeping down to the sea. They stopped at B&B on the way, sampling the well-documented Irish hospitality.

Apparently, a film crew were in Wicklow filming the latest offering from Russell Crowe: the horror film, *The Pope's Exorcist.*

Wexford came next, where Maggie and Joe found a wonderfully secluded stretch of beach along the magnificent coastline. They swam in the sea, picnicked and made love there on a memorable warm afternoon.

The couple then spent a day in Waterford where they did the tour of the famous Waterford Crystal Factory. Joe bought a superb Waterford crystal bowl and a wine decanter. He knew an avid collector, Henry Mackie, who would most certainly snap these items up and Joe would make a handsome profit from them when he got home.

Now, they were journeying onto Cork, but they were going to take their time. They were taking the scenic route.

Joe had hired a holiday cottage on the coast just outside a village named Ballykin, which was about 15 miles from Cork. They would stay there a while before eventually arriving at their final destination.

The cottage was remote enough for peace and privacy, but close enough to Ballykin to buy provisions or visit their excellent pub/restaurant The Speckled Cow with its three Michelin stars and resident burgeoning celebrity cook Denny McEvoy.

The restaurant was becoming more and more popular due to McEvoy's Channel 5 cooking programme called *Denny's Irish Menu*.

"So, what's the cottage called again?" asked Maggie.

Joe negotiated a tricky bend. Once around it, he answered.

"*Taigh Lir*. Roughly translated as 'Sea Cottage'. Apparently, Lir or Ler is an old Celtic name of a sea God in Irish mythology."

"How did you come across this place?"

"Well…" said Joe, "I have a cousin, Seamus Regan, who works for a firm that rents out holiday homes. I contacted him about whether he knew of any cottages to rent along this stretch of coastline and voila, he came up with this place. And at a good price as well."

Maggie smiled.

"It sounds wonderful, Joe."

"It does sounds great. It used to be an old fisherman's cottage back in the day. It's been sympathetically renovated, but still holds its rustic charm. The cottage has its very own cliffside path down to a small cove, where the fisherman who once owned and lived there kept his boat. There are stunning coastal walks from the cove. At the rear of the cottage are some woods complete with, according to Cousin Seamus, a beautiful bluebell patch, nesting owls and its very own wishing tree."

"Wishing tree?" asked Maggie, suddenly intrigued.

"Yes. They're usually found by sacred sites or holy wells. Sometimes they're referred to as 'clootie trees'. People over time visit them and tie brightly coloured cloth to the branches or hammer coins into the bark or leave other offerings. Cousin Seamus reckons under the earth somewhere near the tree is a hidden sacred well, but there's been no evidence of this to date. People come from all over to leave mementoes and take in a moment of peace and spirituality. There's also a lake somewhere beyond the woods."

"It all sounds so fascinating," said Maggie.

Joe looked at her sat next to him, her flame-coloured hair ablaze in the afternoon sun. Her green eyes sparkled with so much energy and life.

God, he had been lucky to have met her and also lucky she had survived at the hands of a cold-blooded killer who had taken her hostage during the hunt for the missing memory stick hidden within an antique clock.

Those dark memories were far away at the present time. They were memories of the past and the past was where he wanted them to stay.

"Oh yeah, I almost forgot. There is one more piece of very important information I need to tell you about the cottage," said Joe, "In fact, it's absolutely vital."

Maggie regarded him.

"Well, go on, Einstein. Enlighten me, why don't you? You have my undivided attention."

Joe smiled at her mischievously.

"The cottage has a great four-poster bed."

Maggie punched him playfully on the arm.

Chapter 2

As the afternoon wore on, they got ever closer to their destination of Ballykin. The scenery still continued to provide a spectacular backdrop to their drive. They passed 80m-high cliffs, hedgerows, dry-stone walls, farms, villages and the occasional ruins of an isolated stone building or a lonesome tractor and trailer. It was all quintessentially Ireland. A land of greenery, myth and legend.

Coming over the hill, a ruined abbey appeared to their left.

Joe pointed it out.

"According to the guidebooks, that is a ninth-century Celtic abbey. Its real name has, unfortunately, been lost in the midst of time. It's now referred to as plain old Ballykin Abbey. St. Columba was supposed to have lived there for a while," said Joe.

"Who?" asked Maggie.

"He was a sixth-century Irish monk, also known as St. Columcille. He's one of Ireland's three patron saints together with Saint Patrick and Saint Brigid. He's also sometimes called the 'Apostle of the Picts' for his evangelisation of Scotland. He was a fascinating character with a great story."

"How do you know all this stuff, Joe?"

Joe laughed.

"My grandfather used to tell me stories about all the famous Irish throughout the centuries. There are some great myths and legends that surround Columba."

Joe loved his history. The back seat of the Land Rover was covered in various guidebooks, maps and historical texts about Ireland.

The abbey was mostly a ruin now. A few walls still proudly stood, but the rest of the remains were dotted about, mostly hidden in the long grass and undergrowth.

"I wonder what it was like to live there?" pondered Maggie.

"Draughty, I should imagine," answered Joe.

As they drew closer, they saw a number of coloured tents pitched around the site.

"Looks like there's some sort of archaeological dig going on."

"Maybe they're digging for lost treasure," said Maggie with intrigue in her voice.

Joe stole another glance in the abbey's direction and commented.

"More likely they're trying to excavate what's left of the ruins before the sea finally claims it."

They passed on by and, in total contrast, now drove by a golf club. The sign read:

Clover Leaf Golf Club and Hotel/Spa
Members only
Private

Joe afforded himself a smile.

"Ah, the face of modern Ireland and the corporate giant."

Maggie grimaced.

"Seems a shame to plonk a golf course next to such a historic site."

"Unfortunately, some people think history should stay in the past where it belongs."

Maggie threw Joe a sympathetic smile and patted his arm.

Further down the coast, a beautiful old black and light lighthouse came into view right at the tip of the headland.

Joe pointed.

"That's Fergal Rock Lighthouse. It was built in the seventeenth century on the site of an old fort. This stretch of the sea could be quite treacherous and many a ship was lost to the rocks around it."

"Is it still operational?" asked Maggie.

"Yes, but it's no longer manned. As with most lighthouses these days, it's self-automated. Although a keeper does come every now and then for maintenance work and checks."

Maggie leant forward in her seat to get a better view.

"I always think there's something romantic about a lighthouse. Its trusty light guiding sailors safely to shore. Standing like a proud and sturdy sentinel. A calming figure in the midst of an angry storm raging all about it."

Joe smiled.

That is what he loved about this woman. She was smart and observant with a romantic heart. They seemed to be kindred spirits. Joe was grateful for this.

He had suffered many dark days in the Met. He had only got to see the worst side of society while policing and soon began to lose faith in humanity. Violence and death became a daily companion for him. For Joe, visits to crime scenes, morgues and gravesides became as common as visiting Tesco or McDonalds was for others.

Policing was not a job that you could just switch off from. Inevitably, you would bring it home with you. You lived with the job 24 hours a day. But back then, Joe had thrived on it. He had been very good at his job.

Living with evil had been an occupational hazard that could blur the lines in your private life.

Even now, all these years later, he had dark memories from his policing days that he knew would never fade. For most of the time, he could keep these thoughts locked away, but on occasions, he would wake in the middle of the night startled and bathed in sweat with the residue of a nightmare lingering in his thoughts.

Maggie Smith, on the other hand, was all that was good in this world. She had a kind heart and a childishness about her that Joe loved. He never wanted that to change in her. It was refreshing and liberating in these difficult times the world faced.

That said, Maggie could be a tough cookie when needed. Her past marital situation had ensured that she could look after herself and also not suffer fools.

Together, they brought the best out in each other. Joe was grateful that she had come into his life. Up until then, it had been pretty dark. Now, each day brought something new and rewarding.

Just beyond the lighthouse, they pulled into a viewing point. They got out to enjoy the remainder of the late afternoon sun and Maggie poured them each a cup of coffee from a flask.

Both of them climbed over a low wooden fence and sat on the grass enjoying the view and their coffee.

"Another twenty minutes or so should get us to the village of Ballykin and the sat nav should find us the cottage," said Joe.

Maggie put her arm around his waist and rested her head on his shoulder.

They both just soaked up the moment together. Life was good.

Maggie never thought that she would find happiness again or trust another man, but Joe had stolen her heart and she had fallen hopelessly in love with him. She knew that she wanted to spend the rest of her days with him. This holiday was only reinforcing those feelings.

* * *

The village of Ballykin was as picturesque as they both imagined. It was not big, but the place had the obligatory pub, church, general store/post office (which stocked just about everything), a village hall and a few B&Bs. It also had a pretty village green complete with a Celtic market cross.

They stopped at the general store named Logan's and picked up some provisions for the cottage. As Maggie busied herself choosing some wine, Joe glanced at the headlines of the local paper and the front-page news caught his eye.

The headline read: *No More Updates on the Mysterious Death of Famous Trinity College Professor.*

Joe picked up the paper and read on.

The Garda at present have no new leads in connection to Declan Byrne, retired prominent historian and ex-professor at Trinity College, who was found dead last Monday in the study of his house in Dalkey where there had been a break-in. Apparently, he had died of a heart attack brought on by asphyxiation at the hands of a would-be attacker.

The house was broken into in the early hours of Monday morning. It seems that Professor Byrne disturbed the intruder and it cost him his life.

Although the house was furnished with many valuable antiques, nothing seemed to have been taken in the raid.

Housekeeper Mrs. Eileen Fergus found the body of the professor when she arrived at his house for work at 9.00am.

The police are baffled as to why the professor was murdered and the motive behind it when nothing has apparently been stolen.

During the incident, Professor Byrne's dog, Oscar, was also murdered.

If the thieves did make off with something, the police have no clues as yet to what it might be. They are appealing for anybody to contact them if they have any information or suspicions on this tragic incident.

Joe finished reading just as Maggie appeared at his shoulder.

"I thought I would get a bottle of red and a bottle of white depending on what we decide to have for our meal tonight."

Joe absentmindedly still stared at the headlines without answering Maggie.

"Are you okay, Joe? Is anything wrong?"

Joe looked up suddenly, realising Maggie was talking to him.

"I'm sorry, love. It's this headline."

He handed her the newspaper.

"I knew this man. He was an avid antiques collector. We met on many occasions at auction houses and fairs. He's also bought a few pieces off me in the past. He was a lovely old guy and so knowledgeable. He worked for years at Trinity College where we visited the other day. It did make me think of him when we were there. Over the space of the few years that I knew him, I looked upon him as a friend. He was always telling me to come and visit him and I never got around to it. What a terrible thing to happen to him."

Maggie put her hand on his shoulder and scanned the headline.

"I'm so sorry, Joe."

Joe put the paper back.

"Thanks. It was just a bit of a shock. As I said, he was forever asking me when I was coming home to Ireland and to look him up when I did. I have his address in my phone somewhere. I guess it's all too late now."

"Should I put the wine back? You don't look in the mood for celebrations."

Joe smiled.

"No, don't be silly. At this moment in time, I could really do with a glass or three."

As they left the shop and walked back to the Discovery, Joe's detective brain could not help but speculate on what had happened at the professor's house.

Declan Byrne had been a scholar and a gentleman. Surely, he had no enemies. Who would want to harm this gentle soul? That said, you do not murder a person in cold blood for no reason. Something must have been stolen, but what?

Also, if you go to the extremes of taking a person's life, it means whatever was stolen must be worth a great deal.

* * *

Driving from the village, it took ten minutes to turn off the main coastal road. They carefully made their way down a series of narrow lanes until they came to their cottage.

It was ideally placed for great views out to the Atlantic. Set back from the road and surrounded by a dry-stone wall, it was picture perfect.

The cottage itself was built out of whitewashed stone and the dark grey roof looked like it was slate.

Outside the front of the cottage lay some maritime memorabilia. Lobster and crabbing pots, a red and white buoy and a couple of old wooden casks with the faded names of brands of rum stamped on them. It added a nice touch to the fisherman's connection.

Joe drove in through the open wooden gates and parked up literally outside on the gravel surface.

To the left of the house was a lean-to full of logs and also a makeshift chopping block and axe (the cottage had a real open fire).

To the left of the garden stood a dilapidated barn.

It was all very quaint and tranquil.

They found the key in a secure key box on the wall by the front door, just under a weathered wooden plaque with the name *Taigh Lir* written on it.

Having tapped in the code given to them by Seamus, the door opened, and they were soon bringing their belongings inside.

Although the place had been modernised up to a high spec, it still maintained some of its original features, such as the wooden ceiling beams and a large inglenook fireplace in the living room.

The kitchen was all wood with granite work surfaces and it held an impressive AGA and a large Belfast sink complete with old-school brass taps.

Upstairs, they found the light and airy master bedroom with a picturesque window overlooking the sea and a cosy window seat to perch on. Also, there was the four-poster bed, which added a nice touch.

The bathroom contained a separate shower cubicle and there was also a beautiful roll top and claw-footed bath.

The upstairs was completed by a brightly painted smaller bedroom.

"What do you think?" asked Joe.

Maggie wrapped her arms around his neck, pulled him close and kissed his lips.

When she broke away, she replied.

"I absolutely love it, Joe. It's beautiful."

* * *

Later that night after they had made love, Joe lay awake in the darkness. There was not a sound to be heard, except the lapping of the waves somewhere below them and Maggie's gentle breathing.

Although it had been a long day's drive, he found sleep hard to come by as he thought about the newspaper story and the murder of Declan Byrne.

Yes, it could have just been a standard burglary gone wrong. Declan had stumbled across the perpetrators and maybe they panicked and left with nothing.

Dalkey, the town Byrne had lived in, was about ten miles from Dublin. It was an affluent place and prone to break-ins.

Regan knew the professor was always working on something. A project of some kind. Could that be a clue to what happened?

He was a fanatic for Irish history and heritage. In his retirement, he had spent most of his time researching ancient sites with the view of discovering hidden treasures or artefacts buried in the ground and long forgotten. Ireland had a rich history of this.

It had become an obsession with him. Whenever they met, Declan always talked passionately about the subject. Particularly the life of St. Columba and his adventures.

Had he discovered something? Something big enough to be murdered over?

As an ex-DCI, Joe had seen people murdered for less. He had no compulsions about what one human being would do to another for greed.

He remembered a case of a man who murdered his next-door neighbour of 20 years to steal his winning lottery ticket. The murdered neighbour had been a godparent to both the man's sons at one time or another, yet that had not stopped him creeping into his house in the dead of night and bludgeoning him to death while he slept in his bed.

The man even helped the police out with searching for the murderer, faking shock, grief and disbelief that his good friend was dead. He had been very convincing. Even when the police finally found evidence that he was the killer, he still denied it.

Yes, Joe Regan would not discount the fact that anything could happen in this sometimes-cruel world.

Chapter 3

The next morning found Joe up early. Maggie was sleeping soundly and did not stir as he got out of bed and quietly dressed in a t-shirt and jogging bottoms.

In the kitchen, he made himself a cup of coffee and took it outside. The morning was crisp but bright.

The back garden of the cottage was a conglomeration of flowers, scrubs and bushes with an old apple tree sat in the corner complete with a makeshift wooden swing. Some basic garden furniture adorned a cracked patio area and in the opposite corner of the garden was a weather-beaten shed.

The centrepiece of the garden was an old rowing boat, which had various flowers growing out of it. It also contained a dozen or more nautically themed garden gnomes.

Joe had no idea of the names of the many colourful flora, but he was sure that Maggie would be able to tell him. What she did not know about flowers could be written on the back of a postage stamp.

It all made an entertaining distraction.

The back garden, just like the front, was surrounded by a dry-stone wall. A small gate by the shed led out into the open countryside and a short distance beyond was woodland.

Joe could hear the ever-present crashing of the sea and also the solemn wail of seagulls.

There was a slight whiff of seaweed in the air.

He sat down at a small wooden bench and put his coffee cup down. Stifling a yawn, he reflected on his poor night's sleep.

His mind had been too active, thinking about the professor's murder and what it all meant.

Since the Goodwin murders, he had relinquished his policing instincts. He had more than enough brushes with danger. Plus, when it also began to involve others close to him, he knew that it was time to back off.

The local DCI back home had made it quite plain that he did not need Joe sticking his nose into his business and that he was more than capable of dealing with his patch without the interference of an ex-Scotland Yard big shot. Joe had adhered to this and had steered clear of any more controversy.

This episode with Declan Byrne was the first time since then that his copper's nose was twitching, and he was not sure exactly why.

At the start of their holiday, Maggie and he had agreed to switch off completely from the outside world, meaning no mobile phones being trawled for news nor television or radio. This was why Joe had not heard anything about the death of Declan Byrne until he had stumbled across the newspaper headline by chance. Once discovered, his natural curiosity piqued his interest.

That said, he was here for a well-needed break with Maggie, and he knew that if he started poking around in this case, she would not be pleased.

They had come to an understanding that policing was in the past for Joe and his new life as an antiques dealer was where he should be concentrating his energies. However, he found it difficult at times not to fall back into old habits.

He finished his coffee and decided to grab a shower before Maggie awoke. He then would prepare a nice breakfast for them both before going out exploring for the day.

Joe put his thoughts of the murder on the backburner for now.

* * *

Shannon Brady and Thomas Cahill stood in the middle of the dig site at the ruins of the Celtic abbey on the cliffside. The watery sun reflected its early morning glow onto the blue sea off to their left.

"They've been here again last night. Look, you can see where they've been digging," said Thomas.

Thomas Cahill was leader of the dig here at the abbey. He was a striking man in his late twenties with tousled red hair and beard along with emerald-green eyes.

His colleague and co-leader was the petite dark-haired Shannon Brady, who was around the same age.

Her pretty elfin-like features frowned with concern.

"That's the second time in weeks. I thought the Garda were going to patrol around here at night?"

Thomas smiled ruefully.

"I'm afraid they probably believe they have more important things to do than babysit a pile of old stones, Shannon. When I last spoke to Sergeant Drury, he told me he would do what he could, but they were busy with a major crime in the area and his resources were getting quite thin. I believe it was some sort of drugs stakeout at Carrickburn last week."

"So, it's down to us, I suppose, to catch these nighthawks in the act," answered Shannon.

Thomas looked uncomfortable.

"Remember, we're archaeologists and historians, Shannon, not vigilantes. God knows who these nighthawks are."

Shannon raised her hands in despair.

"So, what are you saying? We just let these bastards traipse all over our site with their metal detectors and dig wherever they want, ruining our work and stealing whatever they can get their hands on. Is that it? We have a lot at stake here, Tom. A hell of a fucking lot. If the police don't arrest these nighthawks, it puts everything we're working for in jeopardy."

"I know, Shannon. I'm not saying that we sit on our hands, but we have to be careful. It could get dangerous."

Shannon turned away from Thomas. He reached out and gently grabbed her arm.

"Listen, I'll drive into Carrickburn this morning and speak with Sergeant Drury again, okay?"

Shannon sighed.

"Okay, Tom. When the rest of the team arrive, I'll get them carrying on with the dig and supervise it."

Thomas hugged her.

"Good girl. If I can convince the Garda how important this dig site is, then maybe they'll take security more seriously. Now, please don't stress. You know it won't do you no good. Go and have a sit down and a cuppa. I won't be long."

Shannon watched him head off to the battered old transit van.

Carrickburn was a coastal town about ten miles past Ballykin heading north. It carried a small police station with one sergeant and a couple of PCs. If any major crime was committed in the area, the big guns from Dublin would come in to deal with it. Obviously, the nighthawks did not come into that bracket.

Shannon regarded Tom as he got inside the van. After four attempts, the engine finally turned over and fired.

He waved to her as he pulled out onto the road and headed in the direction of Carrrickburn.

Shannon walked back to a large red tent, which was their makeshift office.

Since their dig started a month ago, they had been plagued by nighthawks: 'illegal' metal detectorists hunting for treasure. A small number of them stole artefacts and damaged ancient sites. In doing so, they broke the law and robbed society of the knowledge and understanding that objects from the past can give.

Most of the items taken are sold online, while others are bought by individual collectors. Because of this, people may never see or fully understand the objects taken or damaged because they have been removed from their original sites with no care or record as to their history or context.

This was why Shannon, Thomas and their team were here to uncover artefacts and record them to be sent on painstakingly and lovingly to museums around the world.

They were being funded by the Royal Irish Academy of Archaeological Excavation Grants. Their brief was to uncover more of the ruined abbey and also collect any artefacts along the way.

The local news, press and social media had given the dig plenty of coverage, which was nice, but it also opened the door for any unscrupulous treasure hunters to come and chance their arm.

Up until now, the team had unearthed some pots, plates, weapons and jewellery from the ground. Anything they found was meticulously packed and brought to a secure mobile unit near Ballykin. Nothing of value was left on the site, but it did not stop the nighthawks still coming and searching through the place.

There was also another pressing reason for Shannon and Thomas's concerns. They had both been at one time students at Trinity College in Dublin and graduated some years back. Both of them had worked closely with Professor Declan Byrne.

His death had come as a shock to them as they had been working with him recently on the possibility of buried Celtic treasure somewhere on this site.

In some educated circles, people said that these treasures were a myth and did not exist, but Declan Byrne had been convinced that they were on the right trail and that he would continue his research and let them know definitely when he found out more. He believed that somewhere on the west side of the ruins was a vital clue yet to be found.

Then, four days ago, the news of his mysterious death had reached them.

Shannon and Thomas had wondered whether his passing in such a horrific manner could be connected to his research. If his findings proved true, they could be onto the archaeological find of the century. Even bigger than the Staffordshire Hoard, which was the largest and most significant hoard of Anglo-Saxon gold and silver artefacts yet found in the British Isles.

If this was the case, people got greedy, which also meant that they became dangerous.

The others involved in the dig had no knowledge of Shannon and Thomas's ulterior motives and their work with Byrne. Both of them made sure that they were kept in the dark and well away from any potential hiding place for the treasure.

From the Professor's enthusiasm and staunch beliefs, they were totally convinced that they were onto something real. They just could not accurately pinpoint it yet.

Last time Thomas had spoken with the professor, the old man told him that he had a new theory, but did not want to discuss it over the phone. He sounded excited. He had said that he would drive up to the site and speak personally to them both. Of course, this never transpired.

For Byrne to make the decision to leave his home and drive up here meant that it must have been important. These days, he was almost a recluse.

Thomas and Shannon wondered what that new information had been.

Their main worry was the nighthawks inadvertently stumbling upon the possible treasure. They could not afford that happening. They could control their people, but not outside interference.

Through continued correspondence with the professor, they had built up a picture of where this treasure might be, but the final missing pieces of the puzzle had still been a work in progress. Now with the professor dead, they would have to go on what they had. It was an unfortunate and indeed untimely set of events, but nothing could be done about it. They would just have to carry on themselves and keep the belief that the treasure was here somewhere waiting to be unearthed.

Shannon hoped that Thomas would have some luck with the Garda in town.

The less people on this site that should not be there, the better.

She suddenly felt a heavy fatigue envelop her and she went and lay down on one of the camp beds.

Chapter 4

The two men sat at a corner table in the public house, The Shamrock, just off Dame Street, a stone's throw away from the iconic O'Connell Bridge in Dublin city centre.

They both sat hunched over their pints of Guinness in deep conversation. Every now and then, one of them would glance furtively over towards the door whenever it opened as if expecting somebody they knew to walk in.

The dark-haired man in his mid-twenties was Aidan Kelly. The slightly younger blonde-haired one was Shane Doyle.

Both men were hardened thieves and minor drug dealers in the city. They had been in and out of institutions since the ages of 14, where they were convicted for stealing cars or burglary.

Both had continued their life of crime in one shape or the other ever since, moving onto robbery with violence and demanding money with menace.

Aidan took a sip of his pint as Shane busied himself constructing a roll-up.

The younger man looked up from his work.

"So, this guy is gonna pay us top dollar for this journal then?"

Aidan nodded.

"Yep. That's what he said. We bring it to him, and he weighs over. As simple as that. Job done."

Shane tucked the completed cigarette behind his right ear.

"What the fuck is all that jargon in the book anyway? I can't make head nor tail of what that old boy has scribbled in there."

Aidan grinned.

"Who cares? If this geezer wants to pay us a grand for it, good fucking luck to him. I don't give a shit what's in it."

Shane nodded and took a gulp of his beer.

"Fair enough. But if this guy is willing to hand over a grand, there must be something of greater value in the book, don't you think?"

"It might only be of value to him. You know what these academics and collectors are like. A weird fucking breed," Aidan replied.

Shane leant in closer.

"I wish the old boy hadn't died. That ups the ante from just a break-in."

Aidan's face went serious.

"It wasn't intentional. I only wanted to scare him. I didn't realise he would have a heart attack, did I?"

Shane took another gulp of his drink and wiped his mouth on the back of his coat sleeve.

"That may be the case, but the Garda ain't gonna believe us, are they? If they find out it's us, they'll lock us up and throw away the key."

Aidan reached out and grabbed a handful of Shane's jacket. The younger man slopped beer on the table as he flinched. Aidan got right in his face.

"Well, there's no reason they will find out, is there? We left no evidence at the scene, and nobody is any the wiser that something is missing. We get this money and we split from Dublin for a while until all the heat dies down a bit. By then, it'll be forgotten, and it'll become yesterday's news, okay?"

Shane nodded.

"Okay, Aidan. No need to go all caveman on me."

Aidan let go of Shane's jacket and glanced around the pub. Everybody was minding their own business and seemingly not interested in the two men at the corner table.

"You did dump the old boy's phone, didn't you?"

"Yes. I told you. I trashed the sim card and threw the phone in the drink," replied Shane.

"And you definitely didn't take anything else?"

Shane looked in shocked disbelief.

"Come on, man. No. We came for the journal and that was it, I swear."

Aidan sighed.

"Look, we see this geezer at 1.00pm this afternoon at this address he gave us. We do the deal, and we're away. The long arm of the law is chasing fucking shadows. They have nothing. We're in the clear. Nobody saw us at the old boy's house. No fingerprints and the only witness – the dog – has gone to the big kennel in the sky."

Aidan laughed at his joke and Shane joined him.

"Yeah. You're right. I'm gonna get us a couple of whiskey chasers to go with our pints in a pre-celebratory drink."

Aidan slapped Shane's shoulder in a friendly gesture.

"Good idea. Make them doubles."

An hour later found both men outside a ground-floor flat beside a gift shop named Gaelic Gifts. The area was just off the ever-popular Grafton Street. Aidan Kelly checked his phone for the address he had been given.

"This is it. Number 12."

The grey door in front of them looked weathered and weary.

"Do you know anything about this guy?" asked Shane.

"Only what our source told us. He's a retired academic with a passion for history. He's a fanatic where collecting artefacts are concerned and isn't too fussy about how he obtains them. It's a sort of 'need to know' basis job," replied Aidan, "Nothing to worry about. Just some old geezer with money to fucking burn."

Shane nodded and crushed the remains of his cigarette between his fingers.

The men walked up to the front door and Aidan knocked sharply on it. He noted a CCTV camera above the door, armed with its red light.

There was movement behind the door and a muffled voice calling out.

A few moments later, the door open on a safety chain and the features of a grey-haired man in his late sixties gazed out through the gap. The man spoke in an educated accent.

"Yes?"

"We're the guys who did the little job you asked."

The man's grey eyes calmly moved from Aidan to Shane and back again.

"You have it?"

Aidan tapped his coat pocket.

"Yes, it's here. You got the money?"

The man regarded both of them as if they were pond life and then slipped the chain.

"You better come inside," he said, opening the door wide, "Wipe your feet, please."

Aidan and Shane walked into the hallway and did what they were told.

The shabby outside of the flat was a complete contrast to the inside. It was immaculately decorated and furnished. A beautiful chestnut longcase clock stood in the corner of the hallway ticking softly. On a small table by the door sat a stunning Moorcroft vase, all blues, purples and yellows. The walls were adorned with expensive artwork.

Although both men knew nothing about antiques, they both had enough about them to know that these items and others in the hall were expensive looking.

The man was dressed in navy slacks, powder blue shirt and a grey cardigan. He shut the door and turned to Aidan and Shane. He looked fit and spritely to them, not some old codger.

"Let me see it, please," he asked.

Aidan shook his head.

"Let me see the money first."

The man chuckled.

"Do you think I'm going to part with a grand without seeing that you actually have the right journal? I may be old, but I'm not senile. Now show me, please."

Shane walked forward, the alcohol he had downed in the pub giving him inflated bravado.

"What if we just did you like we did the professor and kept the book and also helped ourselves to what you've got in here?"

The older man held eye contact with Shane. They never flickered.

"That would not be a good idea."

With that, he walked over to a door that said 'Study' on it. He opened the door and, within five seconds, two large Rottweilers came bounding out barking and snarling.

Aidan and Shane visibly backed off.

The man clapped his hands.

"Shogun, Ronin, sit."

The two dogs immediately became silent and sat still. Their eyes, however, never left the two strangers in their house.

"These are my trusted dogs. They are ferociously loyal and will do anything to look after me. You understand?"

He reached into his cardigan pocket and produced a pair of surgical gloves, which he slipped on and then extended a hand.

"The journal, please."

Aidan reached into his pocket, produced the brown leather-bound book and handed it over.

The man took it and handled it with reverence as if it were the Holy Bible itself. He slowly flicked through the pages, his eyes shining. Finally, he looked up.

"Now, what if I told you both to fuck off out of my house or I will set the dogs on you, and they will rip your lungs out? What do you say?"

Aidan laughed nervously.

"My mate here is a bit of a dick. He didn't mean anything by what he said. He was just fooling around, weren't you, Shane?"

Shane was still transfixed by the menacing stare of the dogs.

"Yeah, it was just a joke. Honest."

The man studied their faces.

"Lucky for you, I'm a man of my word and not a pair of scumbags like you two. That's what ten years in the army as a young man does for you. Shapes you for life and gives you a purpose. Now, you may both be a pair of lowlife chancers, but we have mutually helped each other out, so I will honour my half of the bargain."

He looked to the dogs.

"Shogun, Ronin, stay and watch."

The dogs remained where they were as the man disappeared into the study. A few moments later, he returned with an envelope stuffed with money and handed it to Aidan.

"It's all there. You don't need to count it."

Aidan took the envelope, his eyes wide at the sight of the fifties stacked inside.

"Right, that's us done," said the man.

Aidan pocketed the money.

"Can I ask... what is so important about the journal?"

The man's face remained passive.

"You don't need to know that. I may, however, require your services again. Do I contact you on the same number?"

Aidan nodded.

The man opened the front door.

"Well... until then."

Aidan and Shane walked outside.

The man spoke again.

"It was unfortunate that Declan Byrne died at your hands. I did like him and would have not wished ill upon him. His death was a clumsy mistake on your part. But only you and I know who murdered him. So, if you have any fancy ideas about paying me a little visit one dark evening, I have left a sealed letter with my solicitor instructing him in the event of something drastic happening to me to bring it immediately to the Garda. The letter names you both as the killers of the professor and it states that the journal is covered in your prints. I see neither of you today took the precaution as I have to wear gloves. I suspect the whiskey I smell on your breath has made you careless. That was a mistake. That is why I am where I am in life, and you are where you are."

Shane glanced at Aidan, both speechless. When they turned back to the man, the front door was closed.

Shane looked at Aidan.

"So much for a helpless old geezer. That man put the fear of God into me."

Aidan did not reply.

The man watched from the living room window as the two figures disappeared around the corner. It was not the company he usually kept, but needs must. When you wanted a dirty job done, then you had to associate with the criminal element, unfortunately.

To find these pair of jokers, he had contacted his brother Jimmy. Jimmy was the black sheep of the family. He did not go to university nor was he an academic. For some years, he had been a roadie for numerous rock bands. He loved the rock and roll lifestyle just a little too much.

The unholy trinity of alcohol, drugs and groupies took him down a dark path. His addictions led him to mixing with some unsavoury types. He ended up doing five years in prison for supplying drugs to minors.

Now out, he was trying to piece his life back together and turn his back on his criminal activities. Whether that would happen, only time would tell.

Jimmy still had many contacts in the underworld, and he had exploited that fact. The 500€ slipped to him had gone a long way to Jimmy coming up with the names of Aidan Kelly and Shane Doyle. Two more desperate characters that would do just about anything for money. Plus, neither of them was the sharpest tools in the box.

The death of Declan Byrne had been a big mistake, but, in some ways, made things easier as up to now nobody could tell the Garda what had been taken from the house. This bought him much needed time.

All his activity with the two men and his brother had been done on an untraceable burner phone. When he no longer had any use for these two lowlives, he would chuck the phone in the Liffey, maybe them as well.

He now moved to the sideboard and picked up the journal that he had left there.

He moved to his favourite seventeenth-century wingback chair, sat down and began to read the book.

Dermot Leary could not believe that he had got hold of it. The sacred journal with the hiding place of untold treasures in.

From the night his old friend Declan Byrne had showed him it and revealed his alleged evidence of a mindboggling treasure horde hidden in the coastal clifftops, he knew that he had to have it. If the theory was right, this would be an unprecedented find.

If Byrne had discovered it, he would have had it put on display in some stuffy museum. Plus, he would be the toast of Ireland once again. Dermot Leary could not have that.

Byrne had his moment of fame on more than one occasion. It was his turn now.

Dermot Leary was fed up being the grey man. The person who people had walked past every morning in Trinity College on their way to hear more pearls of wisdom from the great professor and his like when he knew as much as the old fool.

He knew collectors in the States or Japan who would pay millions for this horde if found and they did not care where it came from.

All his life, Dermot had been the 'nearly' man. Always a penny short of a pound. Now, it was his time to reap the benefits.

He had lived in the shadow of snooty academics all his life who had looked down on him as a mere librarian. Well, to hell with them now.

He had been telling the truth to the men that he was saddened by his old friend's death, but Declan had become collateral damage when it came to the contents of the journal. The stakes were too high.

He needed to get up to the abbey and find what Byrne had referred to in the journal as the unmarked grave.

According to the professor, it was situated west facing towards the sea outside the abbey walls. The grave had belonged to a young monk named Milo who had committed suicide by hanging himself when unable to cope with the spartan and severe lifestyle of the abbey.

The young man had only been 21 years of age and well-liked by his fellow brothers. They had been shocked and saddened by his death, but because suicide is a sin in God's eyes, he was buried in an unmarked grave outside the west walls near the cliff side.

Milo had tended to the flower gardens in the abbey so, on his death, in a gesture of respect and love, the monks planted his favourite flowers by his grave as a comfort and a reminder. But according to Byrne, Milo was not the only thing that they had buried in that grave.

Apparently, the gravestone now stood alone and unnoticed somewhere in the undergrowth as the best part of the wall had surrendered to the ravages of the ocean. But legend had it that the flowers still bloomed each year and were a marker to where the grave lay.

Byrne had staunchly believed that the clue to the lost treasure lay buried beneath it.

Dermot knew people were digging on the site. He also knew the two people in charge of the dig, and he hoped they would co-operate with him if it was needed.

Thomas Cahill and Shannon Brady had often used the library at Trinity College and Dermot had got to know them well. He had also, on two occasions, caught them on the college grounds smoking weed. But that was not all. He had something else on them. A tape that they did not know still existed.

They owed him because if that tape had reached the wrong hands, they would have been expelled from the college for good and the police would have been involved. It would have finished them both. Their careers had all hinged on the fact that Dermot kept his mouth shut and he did.

Now it was payback time.

The sooner he got to the abbey and discovered this burial stone, the better.

God help anybody who got in his way.

Chapter 5

Joe and Maggie had spent a lovely day in the seaport town of Cobh on the south coast of County Cork. It was a popular and picturesque destination for tourists that was steeped in history.

Cobh was known from 1849 until 1920 as Queenstown. Its port was the final call for the *Titanic* before she set out across the Atlantic on the last leg of her maiden voyage. 123 passengers had boarded there and only 44 survived the sinking.

The weather had again been sunny, so Joe and Maggie had strolled along the promenade and had a picnic on the beach. They then walked up the famous Deck of Cards, a steep road with gravity-defying rows of candy-coloured houses stacked on a vertiginous hill. It was probably the most photographed scene in Cobh. The incredible terraced houses were overlooked by St. Colman's Cathedral and offered some of the most beautiful views that Ireland has to offer.

Come early evening, they ate fish and chips in a seafront restaurant and then reluctantly made their way back to the Discovery to make their way home to the cottage. It had truly been a magical experience.

Joe could vaguely remember as a young boy visiting Cobh on a holiday with his parents, but it was a long time ago and the memories were faded.

As they travelled along the clifftops, the sun hung low in the sky, a gentle reminder that autumn was just around the corner. Both were in a mellow mood as they listened to Simply Red on the radio. Mick Hucknall's soulful voice was singing the classic 'Holding Back the Years'.

By the time they were a few miles away from *Taigh Lir*, the sun had sunk beyond the horizon. As they passed the ruins of the abbey on the hill, they saw lights flickering and moving around the site.

Joe glanced at the dashboard clock. It read 8.55pm.

"A bit late to be excavating, I would think," commented Joe.

Maggie looked towards the hill.

"Maybe it's just people making sure the site is secure?"

"Maybe," replied Joe.

As the Land Rover passed the site, Joe couldn't help but have a feeling of unease about the flickering lights in the darkness of the ruins.

* * *

Dermot Leary closed the journal and reached out for the tumbler of whiskey beside him. He had poured it some 30 minutes previously, but had been so absorbed in the journal that he had forgotten about it. He took a sip, reclined back in his chair and shut his eyes.

He had read the journal through cover to cover twice. The revelation of the whereabouts of the treasure was there to be seen. How exactly Declan Byrne had come about the conclusion was still a bit of a puzzle. One that, unfortunately, would now never be answered fully.

There had always been a story told by many historians that the ruins of what is now known as Ballykin Abbey contained religious artefacts from the Celtic era and that St. Columba was buried there, but the history was confusing and a little murky.

The origins stemmed from when monks had sailed off from Ireland to the mainland of Scotland and Northumbria to spread the word of the gospel and to build their churches, Columba leading the way.

They had headed to the tiny isle of Iona off the west coast of Scotland in AD 563. The monks brought Christianity with them, building the first church and establishing a monastic community.

Once settled, the monks set about converting most of pagan Scotland and northern England to the Christian faith. Iona's fame as a missionary centre and outstanding place of learning eventually spread throughout Europe, turning it into a place of pilgrimage for several centuries to come.

Over the centuries, the monks of Iona produced countless elaborate carvings, manuscripts and Celtic crosses. Perhaps their greatest work was the exquisite *Book of Kells*.

St. Columba and his followers lived on Iona and travelled the Highlands, working to convert Druids and Picts. He was even famous for being the first documented person to see the Loch Ness Monster and send it plunging into the depths from fear when he said a prayer to repel it.

Columba died when he was 77 years old, surrounded by his disciples on his beloved Iona. He died as he knelt before the altar to meditate prior to a midnight service. His monks buried him within the monastic enclosure and there he lay peacefully for a hundred years.

Then, a new threat arose in the form of Viking raiders. They targeted churches and monasteries as they swept across the land in search of riches. To keep Columba's relics safe, they were disinterred. Some of his bones were sent back to Ireland with many treasures.

When the monks returned with the precious artefacts, they hid and buried them from the marauders who they feared would now follow them across the sea.

For as long as Dermot Leary could recall, the abbey had held the myth that a vast horde of treasure was hidden there somewhere, but up to now nobody had ever found anything of note to suggest this.

Columba supposedly initially sailed out to Scotland with twelve fellow monks. All twelve of them carried with them a gold Celtic cross, measuring about six inches in height and encrusted in precious stones. Columba himself carried a golden chalice named the Cup of the Divine. Both the chalice and crosses were thought to be priceless, even back then.

When the abbey was built on Iona, the crosses and other artefacts were displayed there in the crypt for followers of the Christian religion to see and marvel at. It was a sign of wealth and power.

These items are said to be amongst those brought home to Ireland and buried. Many places had been named over the years as their resting place, but nothing had ever been found. The abbey was the suspected number one spot.

Many highly respected scholars had said that the stories were incorrect and that the treasures were buried elsewhere, but no one could say for sure. Others concluded that the whole story of the gold crosses and the chalice were a myth. It had become an urban legend, a fairy tale, but there were still some diehard believers out there willing to do whatever it took to get closer to the treasure.

Declan Byrne had been one such person. His exhaustive research had come up with some hard evidence. Byrne had been the UK's leading expert on St. Columba and had even appeared on television show *Mastermind* answering questions on his favourite subject. He had not won the show, but he did answer every question right on his specialist subject.

The professor had told Dermot personally that he was sure that he had found the location of the crosses. Dermot had no reason to doubt the man. Although physically he was deteriorating, he was mentally as sharp as a razor.

He had gone on to say that he knew the young couple conducting the dig at the abbey ruins and they were helping him uncover the treasures whereabouts. That was when Dermot had found out their names and he remembered them both well from Trinity College. He also knew that they were struggling with the present funded dig at the abbey and Byrne wanted to help them out financially to keep the dig going.

Apart from the two archaeologists, the only other person that Byrne had told about his discovery was his dear old friend Dermot Leary. He had wanted to tell his closest friend so that he could rejoice with him on such a momentous find and help in the recovery of the crosses, but his friend of some 20 years had other more sinister plans.

Dermot Leary was now the proud owner of that evidence. Nobody else knew the treasures possible whereabouts but him. He was now prepared to go in search of it, but he would need help.

Thomas and Shannon were not going to find it on their own, but he was sure when the time came and he needed them, he could get them to co-operate. Unfortunately, it would also involve those two clowns, Kelly and Doyle, again, but he knew they would do whatever he wanted for money and ask no questions, particularly with the threat of that letter in the hands of his solicitor hanging over their heads.

There was, of course, no such letter, but they did not know that. Just another back-up.

Tomorrow morning, he would pack a case and head off up the coast towards Ballykin to start his treasure hunt.

Chapter 6

Another sunny day dawned over the Irish coastline. After a breakfast of poached eggs on toast, orange juice and coffee, Joe and Maggie were fuelled for a day's hiking around the coastline. The weather forecast seemed good, so they were confident that rain would not ruin their plans. They packed a flask and some lunch in their rucksacks and then put on their hiking boots.

They headed first down the cliff path from the cottage. Their aim was to see the fisherman's cove below with its own beach.

The pathway was steep and winding, but relatively safe to walk down. On the way down, they saw nesting terns and also guillemots. Butterflies and bees danced around in the warm air and wildflowers in an array of colours were sprouting from every nook and cranny.

"This is Sir David Attenborough's idea of paradise," joked Maggie.

Joe laughed.

The scenery was beautiful. Being one with nature for a while was good for the mind, body and soul. He had not felt this relaxed in a while.

Soon, the cove came into sight. It was horseshoe shaped and comprised of shale and sand. A small fishing boat lay unattended by the cliffside. On inspection, it could do with a bit of TLC as there was a large hole in the hull.

"Must have belonged to the old guy who owned the cottage," said Joe.

"Well, we won't be sailing out to fish in that," replied Maggie.

"Good. I never was great on the ocean waves anyway. I can get seasick in the bath," quipped Joe.

They both took off their shoes and socks and walked hand in hand into the water along the cove.

Maggie squeezed his hand.

"Joe, I was thinking about your poor friend, that Professor Byrne. Maybe you should take a trip into Dalkey and visit his home to pay your respects. It would seem the right thing to do in the circumstances, seeing you're in the area. I realise it's not going to be the same as seeing him, but it's a kind gesture, I think."

"Are you okay with that? I didn't want to presume anything or spoil the holiday in any way." replied Joe.

Maggie turned to Joe and pulled him forward into a gentle kiss.

"Don't be silly. Of course, you should pay your respects. It seems the right thing to do in the circumstances."

Joe nodded and then looked out to sea.

"Knowing the procedures of a suspicious death, I don't see the body being released by the powers-to-be for a burial any time soon. When they do, we'll be back in England, no doubt. Plus, I have that business trip to New York coming up soon. I won't be able to get back here at a drop of a hat, so this might be the only opportunity."

"Does he have any living relatives?" asked Maggie.

"His wife died some years back and there are no children. He married late in life. He had a housekeeper I believe. We only really ever talked about work. We never spoke about our private lives."

Maggie smiled.

"Typical bloody males."

Joe playfully grabbed her and pretended to throw her in the water. She screamed out. Joe now took his turn to pull her close and kiss her. They then carried on walking.

"I do recall him saying that he had a sister in Australia or maybe New Zealand," said Joe.

"Well, that's something. Do you think she knows about the incident?"

Joe shrugged.

"Maybe the housekeeper has told the police about her, and they'll get in contact."

"You should drive down early tomorrow. You'll be there and back in the day," said Maggie.

"Are you not coming?" inquired Joe.

Maggie shook her head.

"No, you go and do what you need to do and maybe fit in that bit of buying in Dublin while you're there. I'll be fine here. I'll potter around the garden and explore the woods, do a bit of sketching and then take a leisurely stroll into the village and get us something nice for dinner for when you get back."

"Okay. I'll go early and be back before you know it. I'll select a good wine from Shaunessy's Wine Emporium while I'm in Dublin to bring home."

"Wonderful idea!" declared Maggie.

They headed back up the cliff path after drying off and walked in the direction of the lighthouse. By the time they arrived there, it was late morning. They had a cup of coffee as they rested a while enjoying the ocean and the waves crashing into the rocks. It was a wild and exhilarating place to be.

Joe and Maggie mused what a tough life the lighthouse men had when places like this were manned. It was an isolated and lonely existence. It could also be a dangerous one. Many a lighthouse keeper had lost their lives to the sea and many others had lost their mind living day in and day out in the claustrophobic atmosphere.

Perhaps the most famous tale that they were aware of was that of the three Scottish lighthouse keepers who disappeared in 1900 on the Flannan Isles.

On 15 December 1900, lighthouse keepers James Ducat, Thomas Marshall and Donald McArthur noted the last entries on the slate at Flannan Isle Lighthouse. Shortly afterwards, they disappeared and were never seen again.

When help arrived, they found the clocks were stopped and other signs indicated that the accident must have happened about a week ago. Poor fellows must have been blown over the cliffs or drowned trying to secure a crane.

It still remains a mystery.

Joe and Maggie wondered who might have manned this lighthouse back in the day and what their story was.

After coffee, they walked high up on the cliff road until they came to the gated entry of Clover Leaf Golf Club and Hotel/Spa. Through the gates, they could see a long gravel path leading up to a grand looking house. Beyond, they could just about glimpse the green with its flags fluttering in the breeze.

This was probably as close as Joe and Maggie were going to get to a private golf club. Joe did not mind. He was not a fan of the sport. He preferred football, although his playing days were long behind him. He had played for the Met police team for a fair few years as a decent midfielder until a knee injury curtailed his playing days.

When he lived in London, he had been a big Arsenal fan and had enjoyed the years of the so-called Invincibles when the Gunners went unbeaten in the league from 2003/4 under the management of Arsene Wegner. He had also loved the rivalry with Alex Ferguson's Manchester United. Arsenal's then captain, Patrick Viera, had been his footballing hero. Magic times. Never to be repeated.

These days, he was content to watch the football on the television and, at present, his team Arsenal were once again seriously challenging for the Premiership title.

As they turned away from the gate, a grey BMW with its top down pulled up. Joe could hear the strains of what he believed was Wagner or maybe Beethoven coming from the stereo.

The driver's door opened, and a man got out. He was dressed in standard golfing attire, including the tartan Rupert the Bear trousers. He was blonde, sun-tanned and looked to be in his early 40s. The man removed his sunglasses and walked towards Joe and Maggie.

"Good afternoon, my name is Bertie Neil, club captain."

He extended his hand.

Joe shook it.

"Joe Regan and this is Maggie Scott."

Neil took Maggie's hand and gently shook it.

"Charmed," he said flashing her a brilliant white smile that was dazzling, but also reminded Maggie of a great white shark closing in on its prey.

"Are you thinking of joining? If you are, it has to be by appointment. You can come in with me if you wish."

"We were just passing and being nosy really. We're on holiday from England."

"Ah okay. No worries."

Bertie Neil went to the gate and pressed a wall mounted intercom. There was a crackle of static before a voice said, "Good afternoon."

"Hello, Laura. It's Bertie. Can you buzz me in, sweetheart?"

A few seconds later, the gates smoothly opened.

Bertie headed back to the car. He reached inside and then came back with a card and handed it to Joe.

"Look, there are the club's details and my number. If you want to come back and have a tour and a drink in the clubhouse or a round of golf, then you can do so as my guest."

His eyes roamed over Maggie.

"Do you play?"

"It has been known in the past," replied Maggie.

"Excellent. What's your handicap?"

Joe intervened.

"That would be me."

For a moment, Bertie seemed puzzled and then the penny dropped.

"Oh yes. Very droll."

"Do you play, Joe?"

Joe smiled.

"Wrong shaped ball, I'm afraid."

"Rugger?" asked Bertie, assessing Joe's build.

Joe shook his head.

"No, football."

Bertie pulled a face as if Joe had just confessed to being a mass serial killer.

"Oh right. Not my bag. Anyway, as I said, you would both be most welcome to a tour."

"That's very generous of you, Bertie. We'll see how the week pans out."

"Are you staying nearby?" Bertie asked.

"Yes," replied Maggie, "We're renting the fisherman's cottage just outside Ballykin village."

"Oh, *Taigh Lir*," replied Bertie.

"Why yes! You're right."

"Beautiful place. I knew the man who owned it back in the day. Desmond Coyne. When he retired from fishing, he did a bit of groundskeeping for us. He wasn't really a fan of the golf club. He said it spoiled the natural countryside and it was an eyesore on the clifftop. Oh well, can't please everybody."

Bertie was thoughtful for a moment and then said.

"Have you been to Echo Lake in the woods yet? Beautiful place for a swim and a picnic."

"Not yet," replied Maggie, "It sounds idyllic."

"It's a magical little spot. I enjoy a bit of wild swimming when I get the chance. Anyway, I must dash. I've got eighteen holes to do battle with. Nice to meet you both."

With one last glance at Maggie, Bertie jumped into the driver's seat and the car moved off through the gates. As soon as the BMW had passed them, the gates silently shut again.

"Well, that was very nice of him to invite us in," said Maggie.

Joe looked at the gate and then back to her.

"I have a feeling the invitation was more extended to you than me, my love. I think Bertie there wanted to play a round with you."

Maggie laughed at the innuendo.

"You're not jealous, are you, Joe Regan?"

"What? Me?" exclaimed Joe, "Of course, I bloody am!"

* * *

As Joe and Maggie walked around the next bend, the abbey's ruins came into sight.

"Let's see if we can find out what's happening up there. I'm curious," said Joe.

They both made their way up the hill and into the abbey's grounds. The tents were still dotted around and there was about a dozen people on their hands and knees busy as bees, using trowels and brushes to painstakingly sieve through the earth. Half a dozen long trenches had also been dug out.

A tall red-haired man approached them, along with a small dark-haired woman.

"Good afternoon," said the man, "Can we help you? The abbey is shut to the public at present. Private dig. It can be dangerous to roam around here."

Joe returned the greeting.

"Hello. Sorry for intruding. We are holidaying in the area and out on a hike. We noticed activity here and wondered what was going on. My name is Joe Regan, and this is Maggie Scott. I'm an antiques dealer, but also a bit of a history buff. I hope you don't mind me asking?"

The man extended his hand.

"I'm Thomas Cahill and this is Shannon Brady. We co-ordinate and run the dig here."

"Ah, I see," replied Joe.

Shannon continued.

"We're trying to unearth some of the abbey's secrets. It's a well-known landmark here and we've got permission to dig for three months."

"Wow! How interesting," said Maggie, "Have you found anything of note as yet?"

Thomas glanced at Shannon and replied.

"Just some coins, bits of pottery. That sort of stuff."

"No buried Celtic treasures then?" asked Joe, "This site is rumoured to contain hidden artefacts, is it not?"

Shannon smiled.

"So the rumour goes, but nothing of that nature has been uncovered as yet. If it had, it would be all over the news by now."

"Of course," said Joe, "So, have you been archaeologists for long?"

"We've been doing digs for around five years. We're also historians, so we go around lecturing as well. We both graduated from Trinity College in Dublin," answered Thomas.

"Very impressive," commented Maggie.

Joe suddenly had a thought.

"I don't suppose you would have known Declan Byrne?"

"Yes, we did. He was one of our foremost lecturers and mentors. His recent death was so tragic," replied Shannon.

She then continued.

"Did you know him, Mr Regan?"

"Yes. He shared my passion for antiques, and I met him many times at fairs or auction houses. I was planning to visit him while I was in the area. Terrible thing to happen to him. Such a lovely man."

"Indeed," answered Thomas, "He was helping us with extra funding for the dig. He was certain there were buried treasures here, but we have no evidence of this up to now. He was going to personally travel up here to see us, but then the unfortunate occurrence happened."

There was a thoughtful moment of silence and then Joe spoke.

"Did he say what he was coming up here for?"

Thomas shook his head.

"No. Although he sounded very excited on the phone."

Joe nodded.

"We're here for a few more days. Would you object if we popped up again?"

Shannon smiled.

"Well, if that's an offer of help, then we would be most grateful."

Maggie nudged Joe in the ribs. He had fallen for that one.

"Well, we might just take you up on that," replied Joe, "It's been great to chat to you and I wish you every success. If you're about some evening and want to meet up in The Speckled Cow in the village for a drink, then you would be most welcome. I find your work fascinating."

"That's very kind of you, but our time is limited, and we have a lot of work to complete to a strict deadline," said Thomas.

"No worries. Just a thought. That's all," replied Joe.

Joe and Maggie went to move off. Then, Joe stopped and looked back at the couple.

"I hope you don't mind me mentioning this, but yesterday evening when we were returning this way around 9.00pm, we saw lights flashing around the site. Was that you?"

Shannon looked in Thomas's direction once again.

"No, we've been having trouble with nighthawks."

"Nighthawks?" asked Maggie.

Shannon went on to explain what they were and their illegal activities.

"Have they stolen anything?" asked Joe.

"That's the strange thing," answered Thomas, "Anything we find, we take away from the site to a secure holding. There's never anything left, so I don't understand why they keep risking coming back. Plus, with the deep trenches, it can be a potential death trap to be prowling around at night, yet they still come here with their damned metal detectors. The local Garda know what's going on and they promised me that they'd send a car up here at night to check all is safe and sound. We're hoping they catch them sooner rather than later. They really are wasting their time, but the site is so exposed and open that it's hard to keep the general public out. No offence intended to you."

Joe and Maggie thanked them for their time and left the site.

As they left, a man detached himself from the dig and approached Thomas and Shannon. He was a bear of a man by the man of Jerry Dooley. He was a local who lived in Carrickburn. He had turned up at the dig a few weeks ago and asked if he could volunteer to work on the site.

Although he had been with them only a short time, he was shaping up to be a real asset. Jerry was keen and willing. He was as strong as an ox and did not mind shovelling earth or loading up the finds. He had also unselfishly stayed on beyond normal working hours to finish off a job. Jerry Dooley was a godsend.

Thomas and Shannon were grateful for all the help they could get and welcomed him. Jerry seemed a nice man and a gentle giant, but he was the sort of person you needed if the nighthawks came sniffing around. His mere presence could be disconcerting to a stranger.

Jerry had told the couple that he used to play around the ruins when he was a kid and was always fascinated by them. To work here now was a pleasure. With no luck from the Garda, he told them that he would come up to the site around midnight for the week and stay for a while. He had nothing to go home for.

At first, they refused. They could not expect him to do that, but he insisted and said that it would be his pleasure to guard the site. It was an incredibly kind offer, so they took him up on it until the weekend. By then, hopefully Sergeant Drury would have pulled his finger out and sorted something.

Jerry Dooley now held up what looked like a piece of pottery.

"Thought you might like to see this. There looks like there's more in the ground over here."

"Excellent," replied Thomas, "Let's go take a closer look."

The two men wandered off.

Shannon looked around at the retreating figures of Joe and Maggie. Was it just a coincidence that Regan knew Declan Byrne or was he up here snooping around? On impulse, she tapped the name Joe Regan into Google on her phone. She soon got a string of hits come up.

Indeed, as he had told her, he was an antiques dealer. He was the owner of Lost Treasures Antiques Emporium in a place called Oakcombe in the South West of England. That was genuine then.

Scrawling down her phone, she came across something more interesting. Joe Regan had once been a DCI. A famous one in Scotland Yard, London by the look of all the information popping up.

Was this man just holidaying and passed by on the off chance? Or did he know more than he was letting on? She wondered if having this man in close proximity would be a help or a hindrance.

The lights he had seen last night had been Thomas and her checking the site for intruders. Thomas had not had any luck when he went to see the Garda in Carrickburn. Sergeant Drury had mumbled something about maybe getting a patrol car up there by the weekend, but could not promise anything.

Thomas and Shannon were both 100% convinced of an area of the abbey's grounds that could possibly conceal the treasure. Declan Byrne had been adamant about this. They themselves could only dig around that site area early in the mornings before the others turned up.

They concentrated their work to the west of the abbey close to the sea, as Byrne had instructed. The exact location had been a mystery until Byrne had told

Thomas that he was coming up there with the knowledge. He also said that he would bring a journal with him that would explain it all.

Byrne had been adamant that they needed to find the exact spot to unlock a vital clue, but he would not reveal that spot until he met up with them. So, Thomas and Shannon made sure that the others in the dig team were kept to the east end of the abbey. Well away from any possible major discovery.

It was a catch-22 situation for them as they wanted the nighthawks caught by the law, but if the Garda hung around the site too much, they would not be able to do their work either.

Thomas and Shannon now wanted to discover the treasure themselves. Seeing that Declan Byrne was no longer around, the find would be theirs and so would the fame and fortune which would follow. They desperately needed it.

As far as they knew, Byrne had not told anybody else about his theories. They had wondered about the journal that the professor had mentioned, but realised that they had no chance of obtaining this as Byrne's house was a major murder scene and nobody was going to get in there.

As yet, the media had not mentioned anything about a journal and whether it was missing. If this proved to be the case, then it also revealed that somebody else knew about the professor's findings? This would also mean that they would be on their way here sooner rather than later.

Shannon knew that she and Thomas did not have much time to discover the clue hidden in the west side of the abbey. Discovering that this Joe Regan who had been sniffing around had been in the Met un-nerved Shannon.

Maybe they should take him up on an offer of a drink just to find out if he really was only here holidaying or if he knew something about the treasure? After all, he did say that he was a good friend of Byrne.

She glanced towards Thomas, who was still occupied with Jerry studying the ground. Later this evening after work, she would fill him in on what she had found out about Regan and hear his opinion.

Chapter 7

Later that evening over a meal in the Ferryboat Inn in Carrickburn where they were staying, Thomas and Shannon discussed the day's events and Shannon expressed her concerns about Joe Regan and the journal.

Thomas was more relaxed about the situation.

"I think it's just a coincidence that Regan is here. Nothing more than that. I don't think Professor Byrne would have just spouted off his secret to everybody and anybody. He was a cautious man. He wanted to keep his findings as lowkey as possible. I don't believe he would have told this Regan character anything, even if they were friends. As for the journal, it is all speculation at present. I think we just need to concentrate on digging on that westside for now. Don't get yourself stressed about it. You've done marvellously up until now. Everything is going to be okay, I promise."

Thomas took her hand across the table and held it gently.

"We've come a long way since our time at Trinity and changed in many ways."

"For the better?" asked Shannon.

Thomas smiled.

"We can't change our past. Everybody makes mistakes. We can only look to the future. Our time is now."

Shannon looked sad.

"Time is the one thing I don't have a lot of. We need to find this treasure if it is here, and we can't afford anybody else interfering. What happened to Declan was terrible, but it was also untimely for us. We are missing vital clues which he would surely have provided if he had made it here."

Tears formed in her eyes.

"I think he was murdered for the secrets he discovered."

Thomas shook his head.

"I don't believe so. Who would know what he was working on? I think it was a burglary gone wrong. Byrne was a frail man."

"I hope to God nobody else finds this treasure. Not after all our work," said Shannon.

The tears now rolled down her cheeks.

"Hey, hey. Enough now. We'll find it. I promise. I love you, Shannon, and I'm going to make things right."

Shannon dabbed at her eyes with a tissue and managed a smile.

"Well, you can start by ordering me a chocolate brownie for dessert then."

* * *

Jerry Dooley sat at the doorway of his tent pitched at the abbey waiting for the sun to set. He was on nightwatch duty to fend off the intruders digging on the site, or so he let Thomas and Shannon believe. He had another more important job to do and that was why he had not only volunteered for the nightshift, but also why he had approached the dig in the first place.

He had something to hide where the police would not be sniffing around and what better place than the dig to hide it.

The Garda were too busy running around like headless chickens looking for a stash of cocaine, which had apparently landed in Carrickburn by boat and been hidden in a local house in the area. Up until now, they had had no success in finding it and they would not because Jerry had it and he was going to bury it on the site and then let the owner know where it was located so that when the heat died down, they could pick it up at their leisure.

That was why he had introduced himself at the dig a few weeks ago and began working there. Volunteering for the night shift guarding the site was a stroke of genius on his part.

What a great plan.

Jerry Dooley worked for a man going by the name of the 'Ink Man'. His real name was Noel Best, and he ran a tattoo parlour in Cork.

Best was covered from head to toe in tattoos himself; hence, the nickname.

The business he ran was legit, but Best was not. He sold drugs. Cocaine, to be precise.

This latest concession had come by the way of Albania to Italy to France and then across the channel. The drugs were smuggled inside fishing buoys. They were marked by lobster pot buoys, picked up by fishing boats and concealed at the bottom of a huge cargo of mackerel and other fish. It was an ingenious scheme.

Men like Jerry Dooley would then transport them on land to their owners for distribution. In this instance, the owner was the Ink Man. However, somehow the

Garda had got a sniff of this latest load and set about a series of raids on known local villains' homes with a bit of previous. That is why the Ink Man got Jerry to get rid of the stash. He knew that the Garda would be calling sooner rather than later.

At present, the Garda were totally baffled as to why their information had not been sound, but they were not giving up, so Noel Best thought that he would take the heat off.

It was Jerry Dooley who had came up with the plan of burying the drugs at the abbey as he had read about the dig in the local paper. Dooley was Noel Best's right-hand man and enforcer, but he was not some gorilla. He was smart and on the ball. Also, he was nobody's fool. He prided himself in the art of subterfuge and harmlessly blending into whatever situation presented himself. On the flip side of the coin, if provoked, he was a fearsome adversary and a man not to tangle with.

* * *

Jerry watched the sun disappear and then got to his feet. He lifted the large black holdall onto his shoulder and grabbed a shovel. Stepping out of the tent, he looked around. All was quiet. Perfect.

He now walked off to the west end of the ruins away from the main dig and stopped by the remains of the abbey wall that stood close to the cliffside. Nobody had really been digging over this side, so he figured that the bag would be safe there away from the main action at the east side.

There was a clump of wild helenium, a bright yellow late summer flower, growing near the cliff edge outside the remains of the ruined wall. It certainly looked like a good spot and the flowers would serve as a convenient marker. Hopefully, the bag would not be in the ground too long before it could be moved on. It was the perfect place to bury the cocaine.

Jerry slung the bag onto the ground, took one more look around and then thrust the spade into the earth and began to dig.

The ground was hard and dry from the recent spell of good weather. In amongst the flowers as he dug, he saw a concealed headstone. It was weathered and had no distinguishable markings on it. Dooley wondered why the grave was outside of the abbey walls. It was to all intents and purposes hidden completely. Anyway, the stone would prove another useful marker.

It took him twenty minutes or so to dig a hole deep enough to conceal the bag. Digging the hole had taken him longer than he had anticipated. When his spade hit what sounded like rock, Gerry decided that he was deep enough. He now dumped the bag into the hole and filled it up again. He planted some of the flowers back over the disturbed soil. All looked good.

He then wiped his footprints out of the surrounding earth before returning to his tent. The bag would remain buried and safe until the Ink Man told him that it was alright to move it. Where would it end up? Who knows? He was not privy to that information. He just did as he was told and received good money for doing it.

Back in the relative warmth of his tent, Gerry unscrewed the top off a bottle of Jameson's whiskey and poured a generous measure into a mug before picking up a tattered paperback book and turning on his camping lantern.

All was quiet outside and if anybody came snooping around, he had his steel baseball bat inside his sleeping bag. That should scare the nighthawks off if he came at them with it.

Gerry was pretty handy when it came to dishing out violence. In his younger days, he had been a personal bodyguard to stars such as Sean Connery, Peter O'Toole, David Bowie and the Rolling Stones, amongst many more.

He had travelled the world and tasted celebrity to its full until it went sour when he was caught shagging a prominent Hollywood celebrity's then-girlfriend in a Las Vegas hotel bedroom. The star was not too impressed with Jerry's extra bodyguarding skills, so he sacked him and put the poison in about him all around the industry.

This put paid to Jerry's career, and he slipped into bodyguarding less salubrious characters in society instead. To be honest, Jerry did not see a lot of difference between some of his previous employers and his present ones.

He drained his mug and put another splash in it. He looked out across the dig site. All was quiet. He then returned to his book.

Chapter 8

Dermot Leary looked out of his hotel room window at the Golden Anchor Hotel in Carrickburn. He had arrived late last night and gone straight to bed.

He had awoken fresh at 7.00am and got up and showered before brewing himself a cup of black coffee.

He now looked out at the busy little harbourside with its fishing boats coming and going. It looked like it was going to be another glorious day ahead. This late summer heatwave was set to continue, it seemed.

His journey up from Dublin yesterday had been without incident. He did not choose to stay in Ballykin as the village was too small and every stranger would be spotted a mile away, so he chose Carrickburn instead. It was larger, less personal and a busy tourist destination with people coming and going all the time. He would just be another face holidaying here. The town was conveniently only ten miles away from the abbey as well.

Dermot felt the tingle of excitement and anticipation in the pit of his stomach. He was on the trail of treasure, and he could smell it.

Declan Byrne's journal had proved invaluable. The man had done remarkable research. Most remarkable. He must have spent considerable time and money trawling the archives and managing to view many ancient documents and manuscripts, pouring over them and little by little compiling his evidence.

Being an ex-Trinity College professor opened many important doors. Now, if Dermot could uncover the whereabouts of the treasure which he now knew was a dozen golden Celtic crosses, referred to as the Twelve Apostles, he would be set for life.

He had potential buyers lined up from the United Arab Emirates, China and Russia. A bidding war would be on the cards, no doubt. Exactly what he wanted.

The only dark cloud on the horizon was having to ask those two clowns, Aidan Kelly and Shane Doyle, to join him here. They were coming today, but he was not meeting them at his hotel. No. The less they knew about where he was staying, the better.

He did not trust these men, but he knew that money was their motivation and as long as there was a promise of it, they would do as he said. Plus, he had the added insurance of the letter that he had told them was with his solicitor, which had been a brilliant lie.

Dermot Leary knew that he was playing a serious game. The antiques market for ancient religious artefacts was a thriving one, but also a dangerous one when huge amounts of money were at stake. When big money was at stake, then things got dangerous. Even deadly.

From the journal of Declan Byrne, Dermot knew the supposed whereabouts of a golden chalice called the Cup of the Divine, which was supposedly buried close to the abbey's ground. This precious cup would allegedly then lead to the twelve crosses.

Dermot had learnt from the journal that the monks of the abbey who returned from Scotland lived in fear of the Vikings coming across the water to Ireland to plunder and raid. One day, their fears became real as they spied Viking longships in the Irish waters heading their way. In panic, they decided to hide the crosses and hopefully return one day to reclaim them. They were going to bury them in the abbey, but then changed their mind at the last minute. The chalice had been buried in the abbey grounds with a cryptic clue as to where the crosses could be found.

Alas, the monks fled the abbey and unfortunately never returned. The treasures still lay in their hiding places and probably would have done forever if it had not been for Declan Byrne and his painstaking research and passion for Irish history.

The chalice was eligibly the first cup to hold the altar wine for communion in mass that was offered up in Scotland. Its stem was jewel encrusted and it was engraved with a secret message to a fortune.

As head librarian, Dermot Leary had been an expert on ancient script-reading, including the *Book of Kells*. Translation of Latin was his field. He felt confident that whatever cryptic message was on this chalice, he would be able to decipher it.

This had been why Byrne had told Leary about the treasure. He had needed his expertise in Latin to translate for him. His trust in Leary had ultimately been his downfall. Now, all Leary needed was for Kelly and Doyle to dig it up for him.

A text suddenly pinged through on the burner phone he had in his pocket. Leary opened the text. *Well, talk of the devils.* They were both on their way.

Leary texted back, telling them to let him know when they had arrived at Carrickburn, and he would instruct them where to meet. The plan was underway.

Now, he just hoped that those people up at the dig did not go unearthing anything by mistake.

Time was of the essence.

Chapter 9

Joe set off to Dalkey at 9.00am. Although his visit was a poignant one, he also wanted to do some buying around the antiques shops in Dublin, so that it was not all doom and gloom.

He did not even know if he would encounter anybody at the house of the professor, but at the very least, he could see where the great man had lived and leave a bunch of fresh flowers, which Maggie had sorted out as a mark of respect.

He watched the figure of a waving Maggie get smaller in his rear-view mirror until she disappeared as he turned a bend in the road. Joe would miss Maggie's company, but he also knew that he would probably be able to get his visit and business in Dublin done more quickly and be back for a late supper.

Maggie told him again that she was fine at home and wanted to explore the nearby wood for wildflowers to give her some ideas for her shop back home and maybe also do a little sketching.

Up ahead, Joe was nearing the turnoff for the golf club when the traffic slowed to allow a small number of sheep to be herded across the road by a farmer. Not an uncommon site in this area.

Joe watched as the sheep ambled across the road with no regard for the traffic. Their thoughts were, no doubt, on the green pastures in the field ahead of them.

He then noticed the car in front of him, a grey BMW, and recognised it as Bertie Neal's, the golf club captain.

Joe waved out the open window at him.

Bertie suddenly recognised him, jumped out the car and came up to the driver's side of the Land Rover.

"We're in a typical Irish traffic jam. Shouldn't be too long."

Joe laughed.

Bertie's eyes scanned the passenger seat of Joe's vehicle.

"On your own?" he asked.

"Yes. Maggie is back at the cottage. I have some business to attend to in and around Dublin today."

Bertie nodded.

"Righto. What sort of business are you in, if you don't mind me asking?"

"Not at all," replied Joe, "I'm an antiques dealer."

Bertie flashed that brilliant smile of his again.

"Well, I never. I do like an antique myself. Partial to a good piece of porcelain. Moorcroft preferably. The Clover Leaf has a nice selection of antiques itself. Sometimes I'm not quite sure whether it's a golf club or a museum. Maybe you and your lovely lady would like to view them sometime. To be honest, the place is a little cluttered and the committee were talking about selling a few items off at auction or indeed privately."

"Well, I'm your man for that. I would love to take a look and maybe I can find you a few buyers for a commission," said Joe.

"Excellent. I'm in a committee meeting today and will put it to them. If all is well, then we must make that a date. I have a few days off from work at present, so I'll be available around the club. Normally, you'd find me in Dublin in the week. I work in the financial advice field. Many of my clients regularly ask me should they invest their money in antiques. I usually tell them as long as they know that a Chippendale is a valuable piece of furniture and not a male stripper, then it's probably a good move."

Bertie laughed at his own joke.

"You could do worse. If you know your stuff, the right antique can go on increasing in value for many years to come," replied Joe.

A car horn sounded behind Joe.

Bertie turned around.

"Looks like the road is finally clear. You still have my card. Ring me."

"I will," promised Joe, "Also just bear in mind that we'll be moving on after the weekend."

Bertie nodded.

Joe watched Bertie get back in his car and drive off.

Joe tailed him until he finally turned off left for the golf club. He carried on his way and, with no more interruptions, he was in Dalkey by lunchtime.

* * *

Dermot Leary met Aidan Kelly and Shane Doyle in the Mermaid's Arms on the seafront in Carrickburn. It was an old-fashioned public house with a jukebox in the corner and cheese and onion rolls and pork scratchings to purchase at the bar. No fancy meals or cocktails were served in this place.

They sat in a discreet corner after ordering drinks.

Leary regarded them both.

"Right, here's the deal. Not far up the road is the little village of Ballykin and its famous abbey. At present, the abbey is an archaeological site. It's a ruin partly due to early Viking raiders and partly due to the weather and the ravages of the sea. It belonged to the Celtic monks who started Christianity over in Scotland on the now famous island of Iona."

His explanation was lost on the two men.

"Anyway, at the west end beyond the remains of the wall should be an unmarked gravestone. Apparently, yellow wildflowers surround it. The stone will be weathered and probably concealed in the undergrowth there. We'll locate the stone and if you both dig down, you should find a tomb made up of stone, paper and wood. It belongs to a young monk. In the tomb is a metal box. Retrieve it for me and you'll get a grand. Simple as that. And that's your job done."

Aidan scratched a week's worth of stubble on his face.

"Won't these people on the dig wonder what we're up to?"

Dermot Leary nearly choked on his whiskey.

"We go at night when they're not there, you fucking lemon."

Aidan nodded.

"Oh right."

Now, it was Shane Doyle's turn to ask a question.

"Can I ask what's in the box?"

Dermot rolled his eyes in disbelief. He was not used to dealing with morons.

"That's not your concern. All you need to do is unearth it, bring it to me and you get your money. Okay?"

Both men nodded.

Aidan went to speak again, but Dermot held up a hand.

"I have shovels, picks and a metal detector in the boot of my car, so you can do the job."

"Alright. That's cool," said Aidan.

"But how do we know where to find this stone in the fucking dark in a ruin we've never been in before?"

Dermot Leary took a sip of whiskey.

This was not going the way that he had planned. These two were going to blow the whole operation.

"I'll come with you and keep watch while you unearth it. We don't want the Garda sniffing around."

Aidan took a huge gulp of Guinness.

"How can you be so sure this box is there?"

Dermot leant over the table and, in an urgent hushed voice, replied.

"Because of the journal. Declan Byrne was adamant it was there."

Shane Doyle laughed.

"How do you know that old fellow was telling the truth?"

Dermot Leary growled in anger.

"That old fellow, as you refer to him, was a fucking genius. He was a world's leading expert on Celtic history. If he said it's there, it's there. Understand?"

Both the younger men nodded.

"Okay. Take it easy. If it's there, we'll find it," replied Aidan.

* * *

When the men finally left the pub, the digging equipment was transferred to Aidan's car.

Dermot Leary regarded them.

"I'll see you back here at 11.00pm tonight, no later. And be sober. Understand?"

Both of the men nodded.

Leary then added.

"Lads, be discreet. There shouldn't be any trouble, but just keep your wits about you and no blabbering to anybody else about this. Understand?"

Both men nodded.

"We won't say a thing. Promise."

"Good. Do this job and you'll have your money by midnight."

As the two men's car pulled away, Dermot had some misgivings about employing these pair of muppets. If he could dig up the treasure, he would, but crippling rheumatoid arthritis in his left shoulder prevented this. This was a by-product of a shrapnel wound he had suffered many years ago on one of his many tours in Africa. Old age and the weather had made the injury unbearably painful sometimes; hence, the need for the 'Chuckle Brothers'.

* * *

Joe drove along the seafront properties in Dalkey. He was looking for the professor's house. Number 42 Cliffside.

He had decided to take the half hour or so drive from Dublin first before returning to visit a few of the city's antiques shops.

Joe had never been to Dalkey before, but in the early afternoon sunshine, the seaside town looked very desirable. The properties eluded wealth and affluence.

His sat nav eventually brought him to a stylish home with a beautifully manicured front garden. This was Declan Byrne's house.

Broken yellow crime scene tape fluttered in the breeze from the railings and gate. There was no sign of police presence, which told Joe from experience that the house was no longer a crime scene.

The front garden was adorned with many bouquets of flowers and condolence cards and messages.

He got out of the car, opting to leave his jacket on the back seat as the weather was getting close and heavy again. He placed his flowers on the lawn and took a few minutes to regard the others.

Although Byrne had ended up a bit of a recluse, he was admired and loved by a great many people, as could be seen here by the number of flowers left.

Joe was not sure if anybody would be at home, but he thought that it would be worth knocking the door seeing as he had made the drive from Ballykin. He opened a pretty wrought iron garden gate, walked up the path to the front door and rang the doorbell. He waited, but heard no sound from inside.

Joe rang the bell a second time and waited with no success. As he was just about to walk away, the door was finally opened by a smart-looking woman who Joe estimated must be in her mid-60s.

"Sorry, I was in the back garden and didn't hear the bell at first."

She had a strong southern Irish accent.

"You're not one of those newspaper people again, because I have nothing to say to you."

Joe smiled and shook his head.

"No, I'm not. I'm an old friend."

Joe handed the woman a business card, which she studied.

"I didn't know if anybody would be in. I was just in the area and thought I would call. My name is Joe Regan. I'm an antiques dealer. I did business with Declan for years. I was shocked and saddened to hear the terrible news. I'm on holiday in the area and Declan always asked me to visit him if I was in these parts. I found out a few days ago about the tragic occurrence here. I just wanted to come and pay my respects."

The woman nodded.

"Are you the antiques dealer that he bought that portrait of a lion attacking a horse from? The George Stubbs that hangs in the study..."

Joe laughed.

"Yes, that would be me."

"The professor loved it. I can't say I shared his passion for the thing."

The woman extended her hand.

"I'm Eileen Fergus. I was the professor's housekeeper. Please come inside."

Joe entered the house and was shown through to a large sitting room.

"Please take a seat, Mr. Regan."

Eileen Fergus gestured to a large leather sofa.

"Can I get you a tea or coffee?"

Joe sat down.

"A black coffee, no sugar would be most welcome. And please call me Joe."

Eileen smiled.

"I won't be long."

She left the room.

Joe surveyed his surroundings. A large bay window to the right gave access to magnificent sea views. To the left, as he would expect, were two large bookcases with not a space on them. On the coffee table in the middle of the room sat a beautiful Wedgewood vase full of flagrant dahlias. He recognised the vase as another piece he had found for Declan Byrne.

Next to it was a small, framed photograph of Declan Byrne holding some sort of award. Stood next to him was another man who seemed to be slightly younger. Declan was smiling, while the other man was rather stony-faced. Joe recognised the photo's background as the library of Trinity College.

He got up from the sofa, moved closer to the coffee table to pick up the photograph and study it. Joe could not believe that this clever, witty and knowledgeable man was gone. The world could be a cruel place.

For some reason, Joe impulsively took out his phone and clicked off a picture of the photograph.

The rattling of cups broke his thought process as Eileen Fergus returned with a tray. On it was a cafetiere and two cups.

Joe placed the photograph back in its place and slipped his phone back in his pocket.

"Sorry, I just can't believe he's gone."

Eileen placed the tray down and busied herself preparing the coffee.

"Neither can I. He was a lovely man and I enjoyed working for him. He was still such a vibrant character and so enthusiastic about his research and work."

Eileen handed Joe his coffee and he returned to the sofa. She sat in one of the armchairs opposite him.

"I've just yesterday been allowed back in the house by the Garda. I'm keeping the place tidy and clean until it goes on the market. That's bound to happen soon, and I can't imagine there will be much trouble selling a sought-after property like this. The professor's sister, Colleen, is on her way over from Australia to help with the sale and sort out his estate. He had no children, so his sister inherited pretty much everything."

Eileen took a sip of coffee.

"Yesterday morning when I came in, I still expected to see him in his study or pottering around in the kitchen."

She pulled a tissue from her skirt pocket and dabbed her eyes.

"I'm sorry. Things are still raw."

"That's understandable. It'll take time. It's such a shock."

Joe understood this more than most.

When he had been a policeman, he forgot the number of times that he had sat on a stranger's sofa and broke the news of a death of a loved one. The pain and anguish were always the same.

"I understand you found him," Joe asked.

Eileen took a sip of her coffee.

"Yes. It was terrible. It's a memory which will live with me for the rest of my days. Whoever did it also murdered his poor dog. He loved that dog. My children didn't want me to come back to the house, but as tragic as the circumstances are, I love the place and I want to do what I can for Professor Byrne. He deserved that. He was a kind employer. I wouldn't stay after dark, but I'm happy here in daylight. This place has become like a second home to me, and the professor was like the older brother I never had."

Her voice cracked again, and she swallowed deeply.

Joe sipped his coffee quietly for a moment and then asked.

"Do you know of any reason somebody would want to harm the professor?"

Eileen shook her head.

"That's the worst thing. He was such a gentle human being. He wouldn't hurt a fly. I just don't understand it."

Joe was careful with the timing of his next question.

"Can I ask... do you know if anything was stolen?"

"Well, at first, I couldn't think of anything, although the Garda couldn't locate his mobile phone. This place is stuffed with antiques, but none, to my knowledge, were touched. Even his wallet was still in his trousers pocket and his Cartier watch was still on his wrist. You wouldn't do this heinous crime to just steal a phone. It made no sense.

Then, yesterday when I was in the study, I remembered how the last few months the professor had been carrying around with him a brown leather journal. He brought it everywhere he went. It seemed important to him. If he wasn't carrying the journal, it was on his desk and then when he had finished with it, it was locked away in the top left-hand drawer of the desk. He even kept the key on a chain around his neck. It was never out of his sight.

I remembered this and checked the desk and drawers. The top drawer where he kept it was open and the key was in the lock, but there was no sign of the journal. I also checked his bedside table and drawers in case he had moved it. I can't see it anywhere. I've searched high and low, but to no avail. If he was working in his study the night of his death, he was almost certain to have that journal with him."

"Do you know what was in it?"

Eileen shook her head.

"No. He never said, but one day he did mention to me that he was onto a great discovery. He never elaborated on it. It seemed very important to him."

Joe finished his coffee.

"Have you told the police about the journal?"

"Yes. I rang them yesterday. They took note of it and asked me the same as you have: did I know what was in it. They then told me to contact them again if it turned up."

"Would he have told anybody else what was in the journal?" asked Joe.

"It seems to me whoever stole it didn't do it by chance."

Eileen thought for a few moments.

"He was a very private man and not many people visited him here. He did, however, have one good friend that came here monthly. His name is Dermot Leary. I believe they had both worked together at Trinity College."

"Does this man still work there?"

Eileen shook her head.

"No, he's retired. He now runs a gift shop just off Grafton Street in Dublin."

Joe felt a tingle of excitement in his belly, just like he had in the old days.

"Would you happen to know the name of the shop?"

Eileen laughed.

"Normally, no, I wouldn't remember, but last time the professor went to visit Mr Leary, he bought me an apron from the shop. It was a souvenir one with a picture of the Ha'penny Bridge on it. It was very sweet of him as I once told him that's where I met my husband-to-be, Eamon, on our first date back in 1975 and he remembered. I have yet to wear it. It's still in the bag that he gave me it in. I have it here in the kitchen. I'll go and get it."

Eileen Fergus got up and left the room.

When she had left the room, Joe stood up and went back to the framed picture that he had looked at early. He now regarded it again, sure that the man with Declan Byrne in the photograph was this Dermot Leary.

A few moments later, Eileen returned with the bag.

"Here we go. The shop is called Gaelic Gifts. Drury Row."

Joe asked if it was okay to take a photo of the bag. Once done, Eileen looked at him.

"I know you're an old friend, Mr. Regan, but you seem to be taking an awful lot of interest in the murder."

Joe held up his hands.

"I'm sorry, Mrs Fergus. In a previous life, I was a DCI in Scotland Yard. I guess old habits die hard. There's just something about the murder that doesn't seem quite right. I don't mean to pry and if you wish me to go, I will."

Eileen Fergus put a hand gently on Joe's shoulder.

"No, you're fine. That explains your questions and, to be honest, I'm only too grateful if anything can be done to catch the professor's killers."

Joe pointed to the framed photograph.

"Is the man in this photo Dermot Leary by any chance?"

"Yes, it is. That's Dermot. A lovely man who shared the same passions as the professor. As I mentioned, they go back a long way."

"Right. I see," replied Joe.

His mind became preoccupied with many thoughts.

"Did you mention him to the police when you told them about the missing journal?"

Eileen Fergus looked puzzled.

"No. They never asked. Why should I have? You aren't suggesting Mr Leary had something to do with all this?"

Joe could see that he had upset the woman and quickly moved to smooth things over.

"Good God, no. I'm not suggesting anything. I just wondered as his best friend whether the professor might have told him what was in the journal."

Eileen Fergus seemed to relax. When she spoke, her voice was softer.

"Oh, I see. I didn't think. Should I mention it?"

Joe thought about this. Part of him was reluctant to say yes as he had already decided to visit Leary himself, but he knew that it was only right and proper that the police spoke to the man. He had to remind himself that he was not on a case.

"Yes. I think you should. It could be something or nothing. But if that journal is important, just maybe this Dermot Leary might know something."

The woman's look of concern relaxed.

"Can I ask you one last favour? May I have a look around the professor's study if that's possible?"

"Of course. The police have finished in there. Follow me."

Joe followed Eileen out of the sitting room and across the hall to an oak-panelled door that was closed.

"Please help yourself, but I ask you not to move anything. I want to keep it as the professor liked it," said Eileen.

"Of course," replied Joe.

"Right, I'll leave you to it then. Give me a shout when you've finished. I'll be in the kitchen."

When Eileen Fergus had gone, Joe turned the brass door handle and entered the study. He was immediately hit by the silence and serenity of the room, not unlike walking into a church. The room smelt of furniture polish and a very faint odour of tobacco.

A French carriage clock ticked on the mantlepiece above which hung the Stubbs painting. Joe remembered buying this for Declan at Maynard & Sons Auction House in Chelsea, London some five years ago.

Declan had loved it as soon as he saw it and paid a little over the top for it in Joe's eyes, but that was the nature of the man. If he saw something he wanted, he had to have it.

Once more, books dominated the room. First editions, history, art, religion, Oscar Wilde, James Joyce. The list went on and on. Some of the first editions were priceless, yet went untouched by the thieves. This is why Joe believed more and more that they were targeting this mystery journal.

Joe walked to the French doors and looked out to the garden. Beyond somewhere, he could hear the sea.

His attention now went to the desk. He surveyed the top. It contained a blotter and a small cup with an array of pens. A wire lying on the desk also suggested that a laptop had been plugged in there, no doubt taken by the police. Another framed photograph sat there, which Joe presumed was Declan and his wife.

All the desks' drawers were open and empty.

What had been in the journal and was it important enough to kill for?

If so, who knew about it?

If this had been a random burglary, paintings, silverware and porcelain would have all gone in a flash as well. You don't take a random journal unless you know its importance.

Joe decided that while he was in Dublin this afternoon, he would look up this Dermot Leary and see what he had to say. Would this man talk to him? Who knew? But Joe felt that he had to try for Declan's sake.

He thanked Eileen Fergus and left.

As he walked down the garden path, a police car pulled up outside the house. Out of the driver's side appeared a young blonde-haired WPC and, out of the passenger seat, a middle- aged man appeared. He was fit looking with short silver hair and matching trimmed beard. He wore a crumpled grey suit, which he looked uncomfortably warm in. The man saw Joe and his face first registered surprise and then it broke into a smile.

"Well, blow me! DCI Joe Regan... or so it was! You're a bit off your patch, aren't you?"

Joe looked at the man and then remembered him.

"Detective Sergeant Keith Ryder."

"Hey," said the man, "DCI Ryder these days and this..." he gestured, "... is WPC Emma Hewson."

The woman nodded in Joe's direction.

"Emma, this was my old governor when I worked for a spell in London for the famous Scotland Yard. Joe here is a bit of a legend, and I was in awe of him, you know."

Joe held up his hands.

"Enough, Keith. That was a long time ago. I'm retired these days and making a living as an antiques dealer."

"So I heard through the grapevine. A right little 'Lovejoy' by all accounts."

Both men shook hands.

Keith then became serious.

"Can I ask what you're doing coming out of this house? I take it you know what happened here recently?"

"Yes, I do know, Keith. Declan Byrne was a client, but also a good friend."

Joe went on to explain his relationship with the professor and that he was on holiday in Ireland when he heard the terrible news. Then, he told him about coming here to pay his respects and meeting Mrs Fergus.

Keith listened quietly and then looked at WPC Hewson.

"Emma, go on in the house and see Mrs Fergus. Get her to put the kettle on and I'll be right in."

"Okay, Gov," replied Emma as she opened the gate and passed Joe and on up to the front door.

When she was out of earshot, DCI Ryder said.

"I've been put in charge of this investigation. I was on a drugs bust in Carrickburn, but when this came in, I was immediately transferred. A DCI Bryan Box from

Cork was brought in sharpish and is now in charge of that case. The local plod Sergeant Drury couldn't find his ass with both hands. The operation has been a shambles. The drugs are still missing and people in high places here in Ireland want answers quickly. They believe there may be a mole on the inside. They'll also want answers to this case sooner rather than later seeing Byrne was such a prominent figure locally. Joe, off the record, it's a puzzler. This house, as I am sure you are well aware, is a treasure trove of antiques, yet nothing of value is missing and a man is dead."

"Maybe the intruders just panicked and left before they could take what they came for? A burglary gone wrong. We've both seen it before," offered Joe.

Keith shook his head.

"Initially, that's what we thought, but now the housekeeper tells us that something is missing. But it seems too trivial and not something you'd kill a person over."

Joe remained calm as if this was news to him.

"Can I ask what it is?"

Keith Ryder regarded Joe for a moment as if deciding to impart any more knowledge. Finally, he spoke.

"Remember, Joe, this is off the record and strictly between you and me."

"I understand."

"It seems a brown leather-bound journal is missing. Apparently, the professor took it everywhere with him and was working with it constantly. If it was stolen, what the hell could be so valuable about it?"

"I guess if you find that out, you'll find the reason why Declan Byrne could have been murdered for it," said Joe.

Keith smiled ruefully.

"I guess you're right. Then again, you usually were, especially when it came to tracking down that monster Martin Hobbs, 'The Hampstead Strangler'. That was an inspired piece of policing, and I was honoured to be on your team, Gov."

The case Ryder had mentioned was a massive newsworthy one many years ago. Hobbs, a serial rapist and killer, had cleverly eluded the police for a few years until Regan had cracked the case under extreme pressure from the Police Commissioner and other top brass. It had made him a bit of a celebrity. The case had been made into a television drama some years later.

"As I said, Keith, water under the bridge, but thank you."

"Are you staying in Dublin, Joe?"

Joe explained his plans for the rest of the week.

DCI Ryder reached into his pocket and produced a business card.

"Well, when you drive back past Dublin on your way home, give me a bell. Maybe we can have a beer and reminisce. What do you think?"

Joe took the card.

"That sounds like a plan."

Both men shook hands.

DCI Ryder walked off, but then stopped.

"Gov, if you come up with any thoughts about this case, I'm open to hearing them."

"Thanks, Keith. I appreciate that and I will bear it in mind. The professor was a good man, and his killer or killers need to stand trial for this crime."

Ryder regarded the house and then looked back at Joe.

"Housekeeper didn't mention anything of note, did she?"

Joe considered this question for a moment.

"She mentioned a friend of the professor's that might be able to help. Apparently, he visited regularly. They worked together back in the day at Trinity."

"Funny, she hasn't mentioned it before," mused Ryder.

"I believe it just come to her, Keith. The poor woman is still in shock and trying to piece things together."

Ryder nodded.

"Right, of course. I'll go and have a word with her."

Both men parted company.

As Joe walked back to his car, he felt in his bones that this journal held something special. He knew that Byrne had been obsessed with hidden Celtic treasures. In his retirement, he worked exhaustedly on this subject.

Did the journal contain some find up at the abbey? What the couple in charge of the dig had told him seemed to substantiate his theories. And more importantly, did anybody else know about it?

Maybe this Dermot Leary could shed some light on it?

Out of pure curiosity, Joe decided to pay Leary a visit. He knew he should leave it to the police, but seeing as he was in the area...

Chapter 10

The weather in Dublin had become sultry and humid. The weather forecast predicted thunderstorms later. This seemed to be the usual price you paid for a few days of sunshine in and around the British Isles.

Late afternoon, after some buying, Joe found the shop on Drury Row. It was shut and in darkness. A sign in the window read, "Closed due to illness."

Joe cursed under his breath. He had been keen to speak to this Dermot Leary.

Joe dialled the number of the shop that had been on the bag. After a few seconds, he heard a phone ringing somewhere within the premises. Dead end there as well.

His attention went to the flat next door. Joe wondered if it was Leary's.

He decided that it would do no harm to ring the bell and find out. When he did this, he was only greeted by silence.

Just as he went to walk away, he spotted a man walking towards him, struggling to keep two Rottweiler dogs under control on their leashes. The man was roughly in his mid-50s, unshaven and a little dishevelled looking.

"He's not home, Mr Leary. Gone away for a few days. I'm looking after these pair of brutes for him."

The man got closer.

"I'm Patrick Malone. Sorry, can't shake your hand. I don't trust myself to let both hands off the leashes."

Joe eyed the dogs warily.

"No worries. My name is Joe Regan. I came to visit the shop and was disappointed it was closed."

"Aye. Well, Dermot had to shoot off quickly. A family illness or something like that, so he said. Be gone until the end of the week, I believe. Gone up the coast."

"I don't suppose you have his number, do you?" asked Joe.

"And you are? I don't give out personal numbers to strangers, I'm afraid. I'm sure you understand?"

Joe realised that he probably had overstepped the mark and piqued this man's suspicions.

"Never mind. I'll come back another day. Thanks, anyway…"

The man smiled.

"Patrick."

Joe nodded.

"Ah yes. Sorry. Thanks, Patrick."

Just then, Joe felt a heavy raindrop plop on to his head.

"Looks like that storm is on its way. Better head home. Thank you again."

"You're welcome."

Patrick Malone watched as Joe got into his 4X4 and drove away. That man smelled like a copper. Why would a copper be sniffing around Dermot's place?

Although Joe was disappointed, he did have the address, phone number and website details of the shop in the photograph he took of Eileen Fergus's gift bag. He would leave it until the end of the week and try ringing the phone number then.

Joe now headed to Shawnessy's Wine Emporium before journeying out of the city for home.

* * *

Maggie stood in doorway of Logan's General Store watching the rain hammer down in torrents and run down the road like a small river. An hour ago, she had walked into the Ballykin village in balmy late afternoon sunshine. The weather forecasters had promised thunderstorms and, as usual when it came to bad weather, they were right.

When she had reached the village, Maggie had strolled around for a while taking in its quaint charm and buying herself an ice cream. She had found a quiet bench in the shade and enjoyed her salted caramel single scoop while watching the world go by. She then headed to Logan's General Store to buy a couple of steaks for dinner that night when Joe got home.

While shopping, her phone had pinged a text. It was from Joe informing her that he was just leaving Dublin now with a great bottle of burgundy on the passenger seat.

As she moved around the store, the sky outside had gradually blackened and, within another ten minutes, the heavens had opened. Maggie had paid for her goods, but was now confined to the shop. Otherwise, she would be washed away if she attempted the walk home.

The young girl serving behind the counter spoke.

"Hopefully, it'll pass over soon. I finish my shift in an hour and have a 20-minute cycle home."

Maggie watched the rain still falling heavily and did not hold much hope that it was going to subside any time soon. She hoped that Joe would be alright driving back from Dublin. There were some tight winding roads on the journey, some prone to flooding.

Where they both lived in Oakcombe in the South West, it was near the notorious Somerset Levels, which habitually flooded in bad weather, causing chaos on country roads. It was known as one of the lowest and flattest landscapes in Britain. Negotiating flooded roads was something that Joe and Maggie encountered most years.

Maggie's day had gone well. Once Joe had left this morning, she made some breakfast and ate it in the garden watching a song thrush fly down and boldly nibble at the toast crumbs that Maggie had thrown on the path from her plate. The song thrush was a beautiful bird and the most commonly sighted bird in the Republic of Ireland.

After breakfast, she took her sketch pad and pencils and headed for the woods behind the cottage. She had always loved drawing and had gone to art college back in the day. At one time, Maggie had harboured ambitions to be an artist and sell her work, but that went by the by when she met her then-husband Dennis who had turned out to be a nasty and manipulative bastard and stopped her ambitions with his jealousy.

In one fit of rage, he had stormed into the spare bedroom Maggie used as an art studio and took a knife to the canvases she had there, destroying the lot. It broke her heart and reinforced her decision to leave this brute. Now she drew for pleasure and Joe encouraged it, convinced if she put her mind to it that she could still sell the finished products.

Maggie had found a bluebell patch, which was beginning to die in the late summer weather. She also came across the intriguing wishing tree, which she took time to sketch. She then remembered Bertie had also mentioned that there was a lake somewhere in the woods.

After another thirty minutes or so walking, Maggie had found it. A carved wooden signpost announced "Echo Pond". The lake was quite stunning. It shimmered blue in the sunlight and was as still as a mill pond.

Walking to the other side and beyond the woods, she came to an open green with a children's playground and a lone ice cream van. A few mums with toddlers were playing in the park.

She walked to the van. It was named Icy Treats. She bought an ice cold can of lemonade and headed back to the lake.

Maggie settled down to sketch it. She took off her sandals and hitched up her skirt a little so that she could dip her toes in the cool refreshing water. She had been drawing for an hour or so when she suddenly got the feeling that somebody was watching her.

Maggie looked up from her work and let her eyes scan the area. Behind her was the path she had followed to the lake, and it was empty. She now looked across the lake at the trees and bushes surrounding it. There was nobody in sight. Maybe it had just been a small animal in the undergrowth.

Maggie resumed her work, but as soon she did, she felt once more that there were eyes on her. She looked up quickly and thought she saw a flash of bright blue in the bushes across the lake. Looking again, she now saw nothing. Was her mind playing tricks on her?

Maggie now felt unnerved and decided it was time to head back to the cottage. She began to collect her things and found that she was doing this quickly. There now was an urgency to leave this place.

One minute it had been a beautiful and tranquil haven to be in. Now, as she looked out across the water to the dense undergrowth, the place seemed menacing.

Maggie wasn't one for flights of fancy, but after her abduction at the hands of killer Brendan Quinn and the subsequent ramifications a few years ago, she was still traumatised by it all. Although she had learnt to deal with it well, the circumstances she found herself in at present had brought bad memories flooding back.

As Maggie walked back towards the path, she glanced back over her shoulder and could have sworn that she saw yet again that flash of bright blue mixed amongst the green of the foliage. She hurried to the path. As she got there, the bushes suddenly exploded with noise in front of her.

She froze and let out a startled squeal.

A pair of squabbling wood pigeons flew out of the undergrowth and away towards the lake.

Maggie clutched her chest and took a long breath. The birds had frightened her. She laughed nervously and quickened her pace.

Maggie was glad when the cottage finally came into view. When she opened the front door and went inside, she let out a little sigh of relief.

As she put the kettle on, she wondered if she had let her imagination run away with her or had somebody been out by the lake watching her?

The land was not private; it was a public right of way. But wouldn't a person with no sinister motive let themselves been known if they were walking in the same area or fishing?

Later that afternoon, Maggie had felt more rational and relaxed and decided to walk down into the village to Logan's General Store.

* * *

As Maggie continued looking out at the rain, she saw a grey BMW pull up outside. A few seconds later, the driver's side door opened, and a man's black umbrella went up. Somebody scurried out of the car.

Maggie stood back as they entered the shop, shaking the rain from the umbrella before putting it down.

As the person turned around, Maggie recognised them as Bertie Neil. Bertie flashed his winning smile as he recognised her.

"Maggie. It was Maggie, wasn't it?"

Maggie nodded.

"Yes, it is and it's Bertie, golf club captain."

"Indeed," he replied, "What dreadful weather. I know the forecaster kept threatening us with it, but I rather hoped they would have got it wrong."

"No such luck," replied Maggie.

"I saw Joe earlier this morning on his way to Dublin. Is he back yet?" enquired Bertie.

"On his way as we speak. I've just bought something nice for our supper when he gets back."

"Lucky man if you ask me. Dinner waiting for him cooked by a beautiful woman."

Bertie's eyes ran up and down Maggie. She felt uncomfortable under his gaze, and it seemed that Bertie suddenly recognised this.

"Sorry, Maggie. I didn't mean to speak out of turn. Bloody stupid habit of mine. My ex-wife, Hannah, always used to tell me that. I never listened and that's why she's my ex-wife."

Maggie's phone suddenly pinged. She reached for it and saw that it was a text from Joe.

"Excuse me, Bertie. I need to take this."

Bertie nodded.

"Yes, of course. I must get on with my bit of shopping anyway. Hopefully, the rain will ease off soon."

Once he had moved off, Maggie opened the text, read it and sighed. The text had revealed that Joe had picked up a puncture in the passenger side front tyre. He was a few miles from a garage and was going to head there.

He had rung the garage and they were just about to shut up shop for the day, but the boss – a man called Danny Flynn – told Joe that he would stay on and wait for him.

Joe told Maggie that it would probably add at least one hour onto the time that he had originally anticipated. She told Joe not to rush and to watch the roads.

Maggie was still gazing out at the rain when Bertie had finished his shopping.

"Joe going to swing by and pick you up?" he asked.

"Unfortunately not. He's had to call into a garage as he picked up a puncture. He'll be late," replied Maggie.

"Oh, I see. Look, I don't want to be presumptuous, but I was heading to The Speckled Cow for a drink. Would you care to join me?"

Maggie was caught off guard and her face showed uncertainty.

"Oh shit. I've done it again, haven't I? I didn't mean anything by it. Just a drink and a bit of company for half an hour until the rain goes off. No problem if you don't want to," said Bertie.

Maggie now felt guilty that she was viewing Bertie as some predatory stalker. Yes, he could be a bit full on, but she decided that he was harmless. The pub was a safe public area anyhow. What could happen?

"No, it's fine, Bertie. I'll pop in with you for one drink."

Bertie's eyebrows raised in surprise.

"You will? Well, that's marvellous."

He stepped outside, opened his umbrella and gestured Maggie to come under it.

"Shall we?"

Chapter 11

The Speckled Cow was reasonably quiet when Maggie and Bertie walked in. The bar was bright and welcoming. The sounds of U2 drifted out of an overhead sound system. 'With or Without You?'

Back in the day, the building had been an old coaching inn. It had been sympathetically renovated and modernised some ten years ago after being closed for a while. It still held some of its old-world charm, however.

Now with the presence of celebrity chef, Denny McEvoy, in situ, it was gaining quite a reputation and brought good business to the little village.

"Grab that corner table, Maggie, and I'll get the drinks. What would you like?" asked Bertie.

"I'll have a G&T, please," said Maggie as she took off her coat and headed for the table by the window.

Bertie soon returned with Maggie's G&T and his scotch on the rocks. He raised his glass.

"To good health."

They clicked glasses and both took a sip.

"So, how do you like Ireland?" asked Bertie.

"It's lovely. We're having a great holiday. All of Joe's family are from Ireland and he's wanted to come back here and visit the country for some time," answered Maggie.

"If you don't mind me asking, Maggie, how long have you and Joe been together?"

Maggie took another sip of her drink, surprised yet again by Bertie's forwardness.

"We've been together for a couple of years. Both of us came out of broken marriages and met when Joe came to set up his business in the village I lived in."

"Which is?" asked Bertie.

"Oakcombe in Somerset in the South West of England."

Bertie swallowed a mouthful of scotch.

"I remember as a teenager going to Somerset for the Glastonbury Festival. Can't remember too much about it actually. Too much weed and cheap cider, I suspect. Oasis headlined, I think."

Maggie laughed.

"Ah yes, the famous Glastonbury Festival. Still going strong with Sir Elton John having headlined it this year."

"What do you do for a living, Maggie? I imagine you as a primary school teacher or an artist."

Maggie hesitated for a second.

Why had he thought she was an artist?

"I'm a florist actually and own my own business."

"Oh well. Near enough, I suppose," laughed Bertie, "I just knew there was something creative about you."

Bertie swirled the ice around in his glass.

"Has Joe always been into antiques? He doesn't come over as your usual antiques dealer. You know the type: striped blazer, slacks and a pair of glasses perched on the end of his nose attached to a chain and sporting a Panama hat."

Maggie raised an eyebrow.

"Rather stereotypical, don't you think?"

"You know what I mean. He just doesn't come over that way, like he's walked off the set of Antiques Roadshow."

"Well, for most of his life he was a DCI in the Metropolitan Police Force in London. Scotland Yard, to be exact."

Bertie's eyes widened.

"Wow! I knew there was something more to him just by the way he carries himself. Hey, wait! This isn't THE Joe Regan who helped bring down TV celebrity Ron Goodwin?"

"The very one," replied Maggie.

"He was also famous for catching the serial rapist, Martin Hobbs, wasn't he?"

"Yes, he was."

"Well, I'll be damned!" exclaimed Bertie, "The man is a bit of a legend, I believe, with more lives than a cat."

Maggie smiled.

"Yes, he has been in a few scrapes, but Joe likes to put all that behind him now."

Maggie decided to change the subject.

"So, what do you do apart from play golf, Bertie?"

"Oh, nothing quite as exciting. I'm a financial advisor."

"So, have you always lived in Ireland? Your accent isn't from these parts."

Bertie finished his drink.

"No, I was born in Kent and spent a lot of my working life in London. When my marriage went down the pan and my wife got the house, a friend of mine told me he had a flat to rent in Dublin if I wanted it.

Well, I had nothing to stay for, so I went for it. Got a new job and essentially a new life out here and have been here ever since. I live in Carrickburn now. The golf club is a good outlet for me and a place to meet people. My social calendar isn't exactly full these days; hence, the microwave meal for one and a bottle of Chardonnay bought in Logan's."

Bertie picked up his glass.

"Another?"

Maggie finished her drink.

"No thank you. I must be heading back. It's getting on."

Bertie looked disappointed for a moment, but soon the smile was back on his face.

"Okay. Well, let me drop you back home as it's still raining."

Maggie looked out the window as the rain still came down.

"Well, if it's not too much trouble…"

"None whatsoever, my dear. I'm in no hurry. It'll be a pleasure."

"Thank you. That would be great."

At the pub door, Bertie put up the umbrella and sheltered them both as they went to the car. Stopping at the boot, he pressed his key fob and opened it.

"Just put your shopping in there."

Maggie looked into the large and exceptionally clean boot. She placed her shopping in, and Bertie did the same. The only other thing in there was a blue windbreaker. The colour was very eye catching and familiar looking.

Maggie suddenly thought back to the lake and the woods and the flash of blue that she thought she saw. The blue matched the coat. It was almost identical.

A small tremor of uncertainty travelled through her body. She suddenly flinched as Bertie shut down the boot lid.

"Car door is open. Hurry inside before you get wet."

Part of Maggie was searching for a reason not to get in, but she could not come up with anything convincing on the spot.

Maybe she was just overreacting again? She walked to the passenger side and got in.

* * *

Joe was back on the road with a new tyre fitted. The rain was beginning to ease up, which was good news as it was now twilight and some of the country roads were tricky to negotiate at the best of times without the downpours of rain.

He used his phone's handsfree Bluetooth in the car to text Maggie and let her know that he was back on the road and probably an hour or so away. He would be glad to get back to the cottage and chill out. It had been a long day.

During his drive, he had thought back to Dermot Leary. *Did he hold the secret to Declan Byrne's death?*

Joe sensed that this man knew something.

He wondered where he had gone to. It could be something innocent, but Joe could not shake the feeling that he had about the man.

He switched on the radio for a little company and the mellow sound of Don McLean came through with his beautiful classic 'Vincent'.

Joe had not heard this song for years. It made him think back to the early years of his marriage with

Emma. She had been a big fan of McLean and would always be playing the album *American Pie*.

Joe felt a pang of regret. Those days had been happy ones when their relationship was fresh and new, before the cracks began appearing in the way of his obsession with the job and their problems to conceive a child. In the end, it tore them apart.

It was all water under the bridge.

Emma had a child now. A little girl. She had, however, moved on from the father, who had been a personal trainer to the stars and destined for big things.

She was in a new relationship. Still keeping to the sporty theme. He was an ex-footballer. Harvey King. Played for Norwich. Or was it Newcastle? Anyway, for now she seemed happy. How long for? Who knows? Emma could be high maintenance.

Joe now thought of Maggie. Her and Emma were chalk and cheese. He had never been happier.

The rain had now gone off, so Joe increased his speed, eager now to get home to her.

* * *

Bertie pulled the car up outside the cottage.

"Here we are. Home sweet home."

He regarded Maggie.

"You've been quiet on the journey. I hope I haven't inadvertently upset you in any way."

Maggie forced a smile.

"No. I guess I'm just tired. Anyway, thanks for the lift."

Maggie went to unbuckle her seatbelt, but it seemed to have jammed.

"Here. Let me," said Bertie, "It's temperamental sometimes."

He leaned in closer to Maggie. She could smell the scotch on his breath and the scent of his aftershave.

As he fiddled with the buckle, his hand touched Maggie's. It seemed to stay there longer than necessary.

Maggie moved her hand away.

The belt then unbuckled.

"There you are. You're free to go. Alas, you're no longer my prisoner."

Maggie laughed nervously, not sure if Bertie was joking or not. She opened the door, trying hard not to get out too fast.

"Thanks again for the lift, Bertie. Good night."

She walked around the front of the car and Bertie lowered his window.

"Don't forget your shopping, Maggie. I'm sure Joe will have a roaring appetite when he gets home. You wouldn't want to disappoint him now, would you?"

Maggie cursed under her breath as she trudged to the boot, which was unlocked. She reached in for her shopping and then, on impulse, she reached for the blue windbreaker and searched through the pockets.

She did not know what she was looking for, but she searched anyway. The pockets were empty, except for what looked like a receipt. Maggie shoved it in her carrier bag.

Suddenly, Bertie shouted out.

"Everything okay back there, Maggie?"

Maggie was startled, but gathered her composure.

"Yes. Fine. Just some of my shopping had rolled out of the bag. All good now though."

Maggie shut down the boot and walked towards the cottage. At the door, she got out her key and then glanced back and waved.

Bertie waved back.

Once in the house, she put down her shopping and moved into the lounge without switching on the lights and cautiously peeped through the window. Bertie was still sat there in his car looking towards the cottage.

She was startled as her phone pinged a text through. Taking it from her coat pocket, she saw that the text was from Joe. It read that he would be home in about an hour.

She replied to it and when she looked up again to the window, Bertie was gone.

* * *.

After a warm soak in the bath, Maggie felt better. She busied herself in the kitchen cooking the steaks and preparing salad. She sipped on a glass of wine and listened to one of the many CDs left in the cottage for guests to play.

She had chosen the album *Beautiful World* by Take That. Well, the second coming of the band.

Maggie had been a big fan back in the day and had watched them live on a few occasions.

She sang along to their first comeback single 'Patience'.

As she now took a loaf of ciabatta bread out of the carrier bag, she saw the receipt that she had taken from Bertie's windbreaker. It was a small slip of paper.

Maggie put on her glasses to read it and when she did, a chill ran through her body. The receipt was for a

Magnum ice lolly from the van beyond the lake. She remembered the name, Icy Treats. Bertie had been in the area after all and had failed to mention it.

Are you an artist?

Maggie remembered their earlier conversation in the pub.

He must have been spying on her. What a creep.

She suddenly felt vulnerable and went to the lounge window and peeped out again.

It was pitch black.

Anybody could be directly looking in and she would not be able to see them.

The cottage and surrounding area were beautiful in the day, but now alone for the first time at night, it took on a more sinister feel.

She went around drawing the curtains and checking that all the windows and doors were locked. When satisfied, she texted Joe asking how far he was away. She was relieved when his return text informed her that he was fifteen minutes away.

Maggie sat in the window seat looking out through a crack in the curtains and was glad to finally see Joe's vehicle coming down the road and his headlights illuminate the front garden as he pulled in.

When he got to the front door, Maggie opened it, flung herself into his arms and kissed him deeply.

"Wow!" said Joe, "I'll have to go away more often."

Chapter 12

The two cars pulled up in a layby a short distance from the abbey. Dermot Leary got out of his vehicle and waited for Aidan Kelly and Shane Doyle to clamber out of theirs. The only light was from the car headlamps. Other than that, it was pitch black.

The two men collected the equipment and torches from the boot. Dermot had his own torch in his pocket. He clutched the journal tightly in his grip. Within its pages would be outlined exactly where to find the grave. He tried to keep a rein on his rising excitement. Here he was, one step closer to his prize.

The storms had now moved away, leaving a patchy sky with a watery full moon appearing from behind the clouds every now and then. The rain would have made the soil more manageable to dig. Everything was perfect. Even his two companions had turned up on time and both were sober as far as Leary could ascertain.

"Right, follow me and watch your footing. There's been a lot of excavation in the abbey. I have a pretty good idea where to head," said Leary.

"I take it there's nobody still on the site?" asked Aidan Kelly.

Dermot shook his head.

"I've looked into it. They all finish at 6.00pm every night. I drove up here earlier this evening and saw them all go. We'll be alone, except for maybe a few ghosts."

Dermot Leary chuckled.

Shane Doyle looked around him furtively.

"The sooner this job is done and I'm out of here, the better."

He was not keen on creepy places. Ghosts and shit like that had frightened him since childhood.

The ruins of the abbey loomed up eerily in front of the men. Dermot Leary shone his torch to the entrance and spoke.

"Okay, stick close and be quiet. Sometimes the Garda will keep an eye on dig sites and drive by now and then, so keep your eyes peeled."

The three men tread carefully onto the site. The ground was boggy in places and the grass was wet and slippery. They negotiated three or four deep trenches.

Five minutes later, Dermot stood by the remains of the west wall. His torch picked out a clump of yellow wildflowers. Dermot told the two men to search among them for the grave.

Soon, they found the headstone. Byrne had been right. Here was the grave of the young monk Milo.

Dermot switched on the metal detector and ran it over the ground close to the stone. It began to crackle and registered a find.

He looked at the two men.

"Right, get digging."

Kelly and Doyle began digging down into the earth.

"Go careful," whispered Leary.

The moon momentarily appeared from behind a cloud and lit up the scene. The men looked like three Victorian graverobbers.

After a while, Aidan Kelly stopped digging.

"I think I've found something," he said.

Dermot Leary edged closer to the hole in anticipation. He was puzzled, however. He thought that the coffin containing the chalice would have been buried deeper.

* * *

Jerry Dooley walked up to the abbey. He was ready for his midnight vigil.

Earlier in the evening after the rain eased off, he had a meal in The Speckled Cow. He then sat in the bar and had a few pints until closing time and then slowly made the walk back up here. Now, he was hoping to get his head down for a few hours.

He had two more nights to guard the drugs and then the Ink Man was coming to collect them, and Jerry would receive a nice pay off.

The plan had gone sweetly. The Garda were still chasing shadows and soon the stash would be winging its way out of here. Not a trace of it would be found. The Garda had even put out a generous reward now for information on its whereabouts. They had no hope of locating it.

As he neared his tent, he looked over towards the west wall and saw torch beams bobbing around and what sounded like digging.

What the fuck? Who the hell was over there? Random nighthawks just getting lucky or somebody who knew where the stash was hidden? But that couldn't be...

Jerry went into the tent, reached under his sleeping bag and took out the baseball bat. Whoever was out there was going to face a shitstorm when he got to them. No way were they finding the bag.

* * *

"I have something," hissed Aidan Kelly.

"Bring it up then," replied Dermot Leary.

His heart was beating twenty to the dozen inside his chest.

Aidan leant in and grunted as he pulled a large holdall from the hole. He dropped it to the ground.

"Is that it? Is this what you were looking for?" he asked the older man.

Dermot Leary was confused. The journal had said that the chalice would be in a bronze box inside a coffin. The Celtic monks from yesteryear did not know much about The North Face holdalls.

Shane reached down, unzipped the bag and shone his torch inside.

"Holy fuck!" he exclaimed, "This looks like coke. Fucking loads of it. Thousands and thousands of pounds worth. What the hell is going on?"

"It bet that's the stash the Garda has been looking for. Has to be. That's one hell of a load of cocaine," replied Aidan.

"Yeah, but what's it doing here?" asked Shane.

Dermot Leary regarded the bag. This was a sudden turn of events that he had not bargained on.

Suddenly, a powerful beam from a lantern illuminated the three men. They were momentarily blinded.

"Zip the bag back up and walk away from it now," a voice boomed.

The three men froze.

Standing in front of them was a huge man wielding a steel baseball bat in his hands.

"Move back!" he commanded.

All three complied.

"Right, how did you know the bag was here? Who do you work for?"

"We don't know anything, man. Honest," blabbered Shane, "This bloke told us to come here and dig. He had some story about a precious religious artefact being buried here. That's all we know."

"It's true," piped up Aidan, "We had no idea the bag was buried here."

Jerry regarded both men and sensed that they were not an immediate threat.

He now looked at the older man.

"Is that right what they've told me?"

Dermot knew that it would be pointless to lie.

"Yes, it is. I'm a historian who is looking for treasure on this site. I hired these two to dig for me. I had no idea about any drugs. We've unearthed them totally by chance. I have no interest in them."

Jerry contemplated this information.

"If you are who you say you are, why not come up to the site in the daytime when it's open and speak with the organisers?"

Dermot said nothing.

Jerry continued.

"I take it whatever you wanted to find would not be going through the official channels so to speak. Am I right?"

Dermot nodded.

"What is it you think is in the hole?" asked Jerry.

"An inscribed gold chalice. Celtic. Very valuable."

Jerry suddenly saw an opportunity to make himself some more money. That dream of sailing his own little 40-footer around the Mediterranean just might come true.

He looked at the two younger men and gestured with the bat.

"Pick up those spades and continue digging."

Both men regarded each other nervously and then did what they were told. Within ten minutes, they hit something hard.

"Go gently," said Dermot, his fear momentarily forgotten by his eagerness to find out if this was the chalice.

They gradually unearthed an ancient coffin.

"Open it," said Jerry.

Aidan put the edge of the spade under the lid and prised it open. Shane shone a torch into it and recoiled in horror at the skeletal remains within.

The torch now illuminated a metal box in the corner. Aidan reached in and pulled out the intricately embossed bronze box roughly 12 inches by 10 inches. Dermot held his breath hardly able to believe that this box could contain the mythical Cup of the Divine.

Finally, he spoke. His voice was almost a whisper.

"Bring it to me, please."

Jerry nodded to Aidan.

"Do it and no silly moves or I'll cave your skull in, son. Understand?"

Aidan nodded and handed the box to Dermot.

With shaking hands, he cleared away any dirt that clung to it and then flicked up the clasp holding the lid shut. He lifted the lid and shone his torch inside.

Dermot gasped.

There it was, the chalice. Unblemished after all this time.

"Bring it to me," said Jerry.

Dermot looked up at the big man.

"Please. Take the drugs. Bury them or whatever it is you want to do with them. I will say nothing. I only came for the chalice. I have no interest in anything else going on here. Please let me keep the chalice."

Jerry regarded the man. It was an unfortunate set of circumstances that they found themselves in, but it was a dog-eat-dog world they lived in.

Jerry spoke.

"Even if I let you keep the chalice, I can't let any of you go. I can't risk one or all of you going to the Garda, cashing in on the reward for the drugs. There is too much at stake."

Fear resonated once more in the three men's eyes.

"Now bring me the box!"

Jerry's voice was full of menace.

"Give him the fucking box, man," pleaded Shane.

Dermot shook his head.

"I can't."

Jerry moved forward, menacingly brandishing the bat, but he momentarily lost his footing on the muddy ground. This caught him off guard.

Aidan saw his chance and ran at the big man, swinging his shovel at his head. Jerry recovered enough to block the shovel with his bat. He then swung it in a vicious arc, smashing it across Aidan's kneecap. The man screamed and dropped to his knees. Jerry then brought the bat down with a sickening crunch onto his exposed skull.

Shane froze and raised his hands as he looked at the fallen body of his friend. He then looked up at Jerry.

"Please, man. I beg you. I will say nothing. I promise. I..."

Jerry swung the bat, connecting with an incredibly heavy blow to Aidan's temple. He dropped instantly, joining his friend on the ground.

Dermot had seen enough. He turned tail and ran into the darkness.

Jerry lost sight of the man. He had gone. And it was just too dangerous to run around the cliffside after dark.

The big man moved between the two bodies on the ground, bringing the bat down again and again onto their skulls.

Jerry lifted up the lantern in the direction that the older man had gone, but he knew that he had no chance of finding him now. He was going to have to come up with a new plan quickly. He could not now chance burying the bag here again as the man might tip off the Garda. This was not how he had planned it playing out. He would have to find another hiding place.

* * *

Dermot ran out onto the cliffside. He had his torch, and he negotiated his way along the pathway. He knew that if he followed the path in a circular fashion, he would come back to where he had parked his car. Once there, he could escape.

As much as he had despised Aidan and Shane, he shuddered at what had happened to them. In his favour, there was now no witnesses to the finding of the chalice or the murder of Byrne. The man with the drugs was hardly going to call the Garda now, was he? Slowly and quietly, he walked on, clutching the box tightly to his chest.

* * *

Jerry dragged the bodies of the two men a short distance to the cliff's edge and dumped them one by one without ceremony into the wild sea below. With the strong currents on this part of the coast, the bodies would be washed away without a trace. Using a spade, he filled in the hole. He then covered up the footprints and any evidence of blood. He picked up the spades, bat, metal detector and discarded torches and disposed of them in the sea as well. When he was satisfied that everything had been got rid of, he walked back for a final check on the scene of his crime.

He felt no remorse. It had to be done. This drugs operation was a lot bigger than him and his boss. He could not fuck it up in any shape or form.

He now pulled out his phone and made a call. After a dozen rings, an irritated and sleepy voice answered.

"What the fuck is it? Do you know what time it is?"

"Listen up, Noel. Things have taken a turn for the worse up at the abbey. I've got to get the bag to you straight away. Can we meet?"

After the call, Jerry packed up his tent and belongings and put them in his van along with the holdall. That was when he spied a leather-bound journal on the grass. He picked it up and flicked through it. Inside was a series of scribbles, diagrams, drawings and numbers. It made no sense to Jerry, and it was not of any use to him. He tossed the book into the wildflowers.

Jerry had arranged to meet the Ink Man at a rendezvous point named Kelly's Stone in an hour. It was an ancient rocking stone, also known as a logan. It was a well-known landmark on the Dublin to Cork coastal road.

This stone and its like were thought to have occurred during the Ice Age. However, lots of the common rocking stones seen across the British Isles were likely a result of extreme weather or weathering over time. Rocking stones are aptly named; they are described as huge boulders, which are balanced enough to be able to rock when pressure is applied.

Noel Best, aka the Ink Man, had not been happy to have his sleep disturbed to find out that his plans would have to change. When he met Jerry, he had some explaining to do.

***

Dermot Leary made it back to his car safely. He jumped in and put the box down on the floor in the passenger footwell.

He breathed a sigh of relief.

The chalice was his. Once he got it back to his hotel, he would inspect it for the hidden clue that he needed to solve the next part of the mystery. The journal would help.

Shit.

He realised in his haste to get away from the big guy with the bat that he had left the journal by the grave back at the abbey. Christ, what a fool.

He sat still, running this fact through his head and trying to figure out the best solution.

Dermot knew that he could not risk going back to the abbey now. Not with that lunatic up there. He would have to come back early tomorrow and see if he could retrieve it.

But what if it rained? The book would be ruined. The secrets lost forever.

He began to panic and then the realisation hit him. The journal had served its purpose. It had got him the chalice.

The clue to the crosses' whereabouts were now on the sacred cup, not in the journal.

He would still have to come back early tomorrow and find it. It was evidence that he could not let fall into the wrong hands.

He now glanced at the car that the two men had drove to the abbey in. If it was left here, the Garda would be sniffing around. That would not do, not now that he was in touching distance of his prize.

Glancing around to make sure that all was quiet, he got out of his car and went to the boot. He had a half-filled can of petrol in there that he always carried for emergencies.

He moved to the other car, picked up a rock from the ground and used it to smash a side window. He then proceeded to pour the petrol inside the car and finished by using the remainder on the outside.

Reaching in his pocket, he produced a pocketbook of matches and lit it before chucking the matchbox into the car. It immediately went up like an inferno.

Dermot Leary returned the can to his boot and got back into his car. He did a U-turn on the quiet road and headed back towards Carrickburn. A few minutes later, he heard the faint explosion as the petrol on the car ignited.

Although Dermot wanted to speed away from the site of the fire, he controlled the impulse and kept to the road speed limits. He did not want to get pulled over.

He glanced into the footwell at the box and his face broke into a wide grin. Not long now and he would be richer than beyond his wildest dreams.

He had always wanted to live in the Far East. Thailand maybe or Cambodia. He wanted to learn about a different culture and way of life. Also, he wanted to disappear for good. This dream was rapidly becoming a reality, but he had to act fast.

He knew that the Garda must be wanting to speak to him about Declan Byrne by now. Mrs Fergus, the housekeeper, must have told them that he had been a close friend of the professor. Soon they would begin to look for him. If he kept one step ahead, he would be out of the country soon and safe.

Chapter 13

The next morning, the storm had cleared the air and it was another glorious day. Joe and Maggie were enjoying breakfast in the garden once more. Both were oblivious to the fact that they had had an intruder on the property in the night.

The previous evening, over a beautiful steak dinner and a great bottle of wine, Maggie had told Joe about the strange encounter with Bertie and her suspicions that he had been spying on her at the lake. She also told him about the receipt in the jacket. Joe was not happy and said that he would have it out with the man.

Maggie pacified him for the night, but Joe could not sleep with his thoughts in turmoil. The man had known that he was away in Dublin and that Maggie was alone and he had premeditatedly gone looking for her like some sexual predator. Joe had dealt with enough of them in the past to understand their warped logic.

Early the next morning, he had slipped out of bed and moved to the living room where he texted an old contact from the police, Sally Ingram, asking her to run a check on Bertie Neil. Later, as Maggie prepared breakfast, he received a text back from Ingram informing him that there were no past convictions on Neil, except for a few parking offences.

Joe digested this information.

So, Bertie had no offences against him or was it that he was too clever not to have been caught? The jury was out at present. Maybe he was just a 'chancer' who thought that he would try his luck?

Now, as Joe sipped his coffee, he reflected on the situation.

"This is what we do. Bertie invited us for lunch and to view the surplus antiques at the golf club. I suggest that we take him up on this offer today and while I'm there, I'll have a quiet word with him."

"Do we have to, Joe? We're leaving for Cork in a few days and will probably never see the man again. I don't want any trouble," said Maggie as she spooned strawberry jam onto her croissant.

"There won't be any trouble. I'll just have a quiet word. That's all. It may deter him from trying it on with the next female he meets."

"Well, in that case, I'd rather not be there. It'll be embarrassing for me," replied Maggie.

"What will you do then?"

"I'll go to the lake and finish my sketch."

Joe looked at Maggie over the rim of his coffee mug.

"Won't you be scared?"

Maggie smiled.

"Not if you're at the golf club with Captain Slime. No, I'll be fine."

"Okay. I'll phone him then," answered Joe.

Joe pulled out his phone and punched in the number that Bertie had given him on his business card. After two rings, Bertie answered.

"Hello?"

"Bertie, it's Joe Regan."

There was a moment's silence. Then, Bertie spoke.

"Joe! Nice to hear from you. How can I help?"

"I wondered if today would be okay to come over and view the antiques you mentioned."

Bertie seemed flustered.

"Today, you say? Might be a bit awkward."

Joe heard the apprehension in his voice.

"Shame if you can't as we're moving on to Cork in a few days," Joe said.

"Okay. Right. No, it'll be fine. Come over for 1.00pm and have a spot of lunch and we can go from there."

There was another awkward silence.

"Will Maggie be with you?"

Joe breathed deeply.

"No, I'm afraid she's busy. She's sketching the lake behind our cottage. Did you know she's a pretty handy artist?"

"No. I had no idea. Anyway, I'll see you at 1.00pm."

Joe hung up and reached for his slice of toast and marmite.

"All sorted. I'm meeting him at 1300 hours."

Maggie apprehensively sipped her coffee.

"You will behave, won't you, Joe?" she asked.

"Scout's honour, Miss. I promise," replied Joe.

* * *

Jerry Dooley had met with Noel Best and explained what had happened at the site. Noel had not been a happy man and told Jerry that he would have to hang onto the bag another few days because the Garda were breathing down his neck and his contact with the boat was not yet ready to move.

Jerry told him that he could not chance burying it at the abbey anymore as it was now too dangerous. The Ink Man replied that he did not care where the stash was hidden as long as it was safe for another 48 hours. Then, he would take care of it. Under no circumstances was Jerry to bring it back to Carrickburn or Noel's own place because the Garda were still swarming all over.

Jerry realised that it was pointless arguing with the boss as he was not going to win. Plus, if he pissed him off enough, he would end up with a bullet in his head.

Noel Best quizzed him about the men at the abbey and asked if Jerry was sure that they had come across the bag by accident. Jerry assured him that was the case and that they were no longer a threat.

Best then asked about the man who got away. Jerry again told him that the man was more interested in an ancient chalice than a bag of drugs. He was a historian, not a crook. He was confident that he would not cause trouble. They had both made off with what they wanted, and he was adamant that their paths would not cross again.

The Ink Man told Jerry in no uncertain terms that he had better be right as he could not afford any fuckups on his drugs deal. He was dealing with some heavy-duty characters.

"Find another safe place for the bag so that the Garda will never discover it and then lay low. I'll call you when things are ready to roll. Understand?"

Jerry nodded.

"Don't fuck this up, Jerry. I'm warning you," said Best.

After the meet, Jerry had headed back home in his van with the holdall hidden under a load of camping stuff in the back. The time was 3.00am and still dark.

He was sure that the police were not onto him at present because his relationship with the Ink Man was on a purely need-to-know basis. They did not hang out together socially. Most of their work was conducted by phone.

To most people in Carrickburn where he lived, Jerry was a local handyman and gentle giant. They knew nothing of his other life. His immediate problem was finding a home for the bag as soon as possible. He could not hang onto it much longer.

As he rounded a bend, he noticed the fisherman's cottage *Taigh Lir* to his right, which used to be owned by Desmond Coyne. Jerry had been good friends with Desmond while he was alive. They had shared many a Guinness and done a bit of fishing now and again too.

Jerry had also done some work around the place and knew the layout. He particularly remembered the large outhouse in the garden with its many nooks and crannies. *A perfect hiding place for the bag?*

Jerry knew that this was now a holiday rental cottage. People came and went, but it was never occupied permanently.

There was a 4X4 in the drive and all the curtains were still drawn. Jerry pondered if he should hide the bag here. He just could not ride around with it as the Garda had been doing regular stop and spot checks on vehicles along the roads from Dublin to Cork. It was risky to be driving with the bag. He would feel a whole lot better if he offloaded it.

Jerry pulled over just a little down the road from *Taigh Lir* and killed the headlights. He got out the bag and stealthily made his way to the cottage. He threw the bag over the fence onto the grass and climbed over himself.

All was quiet, except for the sea crashing into the cove across the way and the haunting hoot of an owl somewhere close by. Minutes later, Jerry was inside the outhouse. He remembered that it was never padlocked, only bolted, and he was pleased to find it still that way.

Inside the area was big and contained rusty bits of machinery that no longer looked like they worked. There was a tractor, lawnmowers, an old fridge and freezer, empty oil drums, fishing nets, garden tools and general rubbish.

He saw a wooden ladder leading up into what looked like a loft space. Jerry tested the ladder. It seemed firm. Grabbing the bag, he ascended and got into the space. Once more, this area was cluttered with rubbish.

Jerry went to the eaves in the roof and found space to push the bag into. It was well concealed there in the corner in the darkness. He felt happy this time that it would be safe. He would come back for it soon. He could not imagine the people in the cottage at present venturing up into the loft for any good reason while they were on holiday.

As he pulled away from the cottage, he smiled with satisfaction. Everything was back on course and, come the weekend, he would be far away from here enjoying an exotic holiday in the sun.

* * *

Thomas Cahill and Shannon Brady had decided to get up to the dig site at the abbey earlier than the others. They wanted to do a bit of digging themselves that was not on the agenda.

They noticed Jerry had packed up his tent and gone home. He had not phoned them in the night, so all must have been quiet with no more visitations from nighthawks.

Shannon rang his number just to doublecheck, but it went to answerphone. They both now headed to the west wall carrying spades. They were determined to find whatever was hidden in this area.

As they reached the remains of the wall and walked to the cliffside, Shannon was drawn to the bright yellow flowers. As she got closer, she saw a book lying amongst them. Intrigued, she picked it up.

"What have you there?" asked Thomas.

"Not sure. Some sort of journal by the looks of it."

Shannon opened the book to the first page and gasped when she read the name on the inside cover.

"What is it?" asked Thomas.

"Look!" replied Shannon in shock.

Thomas moved closer and read what Shannon was pointing at.

This journal belongs to Professor Declan Byrne.

"Shit. I don't believe it. Is this real or some sort of prank?"

Shannon flicked through the pages.

"It looks real, Tom. Is this the professor's journal with the secrets to the whereabouts of the hidden treasure?"

Thomas shook his head.

"But how the hell did it get here? I don't understand. Has the professor brought it from beyond the grave? I don't get it..."

Suddenly, a voice sounded behind them.

"Maybe I can help answer that question."

Both were startled and turned around to see an elderly man standing there.

They both immediately recognised him as Dermot Leary, the librarian who had worked at Trinity College when they studied there. They wondered what he was doing here.

Suddenly, their day had got worse.

* * *

The previous evening when Dermot Leary was back safely at his hotel, he had studied the chalice with infinite care. The box it had been in had preserved it beautifully. The gold was not blemished in any way and the jewels encrusted in it shone brightly after he had cleaned and polished it up.

Now, with the help of a magnifier called a loupe attached to his eye, he scoured the chalice for markings. It did not take him long to discover a small group of words engraved in Latin on the bottom of the chalice. How fortunate that he had a Master's degree in the language.

Duodecim Apostolis in prope speluncam latent nisi inventi fuerint in mari

As he read the inscription, he wrote in down in English on a notepad.

The twelve apostles are hiding in a cave nearby. If not discovered, they will be taken by the sea forever.

So, the crosses had been hidden in a cave in the cliffside somewhere.

According to Byrne's journal, there used to be a small stone chapel on the clifftops somewhere in the vicinity of the abbey. It was a place of sanctuary and prayer with stunning views out to sea. The chapel could only accommodate three to four people.

It was said that there was a secret passage in its floor that led down into the cliffs to a subterranean cavern where the monks had hidden their most prized treasures. The Celtic crosses.

When the Vikings had finally captured the abbey and plundered it, the crosses were well protected and not within its walls. How clever and resourceful. The monks hid them, knowing that they probably would never be back for them, but hoped that they would be found sometime in the future.

The chapel was no longer on the clifftops. The weather and the sea had taken it a long time ago, but somewhere on the cliffs was a sea cave, which supposedly led up into the cavern from the beach below.

Although Byrne had discovered this vital piece of evidence, he had not written which cove along the coast might hide the cave. This was something that Leary was going to have to discover himself.

The chalice had been the key to confirming Byrne's findings. Buried once more near to the abbey, but in the unmarked grave of the young monk just outside the walls. The grave lay unnoticed and unattended so nobody ever knew its secret.

That was until through his extensive research and obsession, Declan Byrne had found evidence of it written down somewhere in the archives and cracked the code.

Good old Declan.

Now, it was time for Dermot to claim the next part of the prize, but he needed the journal back.

The coastline was a long and treacherous one, but he felt that the crosses would not have been hidden too far from the abbey.

He decided to go up to the abbey and reacquaint himself with the two in charge of the dig and see if he could enlist their help to uncover the crosses, now that 'Laurel and Hardy' were no longer around. He needed a bit of young muscle. He was not as young as he used to be and years of sitting on his ass had begun to soften him.

If they complied, he would then think of a way to get rid of them both later. For now, he needed to think of a viable story that they would believe.

***

"It's incredible," said Thomas, "Truly incredible."

He was holding the chalice and marvelling at it. The three of them were seated in the main tent on site.

"This is the legendary Cup of the Divine, which St. Columba performed communion with," explained Dermot.

"I've heard of it, but I didn't believe it existed," exclaimed Shannon.

"As I said, dear Declan told me of his discovery and how he planned to come here to unearth the treasures himself, but something spooked him. Spooked him enough to give me the book for safekeeping. He said that he thought somebody was watching him. Alas, he was right, poor man. He entrusted me with the journal and the secret. I should have given it to the police, but this is a major find. Worth millions. A chance like this just doesn't come around in a lifetime.

I own up. I came up here last night truly excited of the prospect of finding the chalice. I hadn't realised that you both were in charge of the dig. Otherwise, I wouldn't have come here uninvited. But you must understand, I wasn't thinking straight. We all make mistakes, don't we?"

He left the statement hanging heavy in the air.

"So, I came here last night to the site where Declan believed the chalice to be, and I found it. In my haste to take it away, I left the journal behind."

"We had a man camping here last night watching the site. I don't understand why he didn't see you," said Thomas.

Dermot licked his lips nervously.

"Have you asked him?"

Shannon shook her head.

"He's not here and not answering his phone."

Dermot inwardly breathed a sigh of relief. For now, his story held up.

"Rest assured, he was here, and he chased me. That's why I forgot the journal, but I got away."

Momentarily, he wondered whether he should mention about the drugs and their man being a crook and a killer, but he thought that might scare them off and get them to involve the Garda, so he kept quiet. He had a feeling that the big fella and his stash would not be around here again. He had used the site for his own gains, not for the love of history.

"So, Dermot, if you hadn't left the journal behind, I take it you would have made away with the chalice?" asked Thomas.

Dermot hung his head in fake shame.

"Alas, yes, I might have done, but you see, the chalice is a key to other treasures and their whereabouts."

"What other treasures?" asked Shannon.

"The twelve Celtic crosses carried by St. Columba's fellow monks," answered Dermot.

Thomas and Shannon glanced at each other and then looked at Dermot.

"Do you know their whereabouts?"

Dermot Leary nodded.

"I believe I do, but I need the journal to confirm it. Plus, I need help to find them."

Thomas looked at him.

"Technically, I should call the police on you. Also, anything found on this site goes through us."

Dermot hedged his bets.

"True enough. But we have history, don't we? You wouldn't be here in this position of authority without my help, would you? I've come to collect the debt you both owe me."

Thomas smiled.

"You have no proof of that debt anymore. It's in the past."

"Is that right?" replied Dermot.

* * *

Back in their university days, Thomas and Shannon had enjoyed smoking weed, but got themselves into a spot of bother when they ended up owing a dealer money which they did not have. Things were looking bad as this dealer was a nasty sort.

Thomas and Shannon had struck up a friendship with Dermot over their years in Trinity. Out of desperation, they had gone to him for advice.

Dermot told them that he had an old army buddy that could help them out if they were really down on their luck, but it might involve something that they were not necessarily comfortable with. His friend made low-budget adult porn films for the foreign market and paid good money if they were up for starring in one.

Thomas and Shannon were rock bottom, so they agreed. It was not their finest hour, but it got the dealer off their backs. Apart from the man who filmed it, Dermot was the only other person who knew about it. He promised to keep it a secret. That was until now.

"Remember your little film debut with my friend Rusty?" continued Dermot, "Of course, you do. How could you forget? If that secret had got out, your careers would have been down the pan."

Thomas swallowed hard.

"You promised us, Dermot, that you would tell nobody. You gave us the master tape back, so there's no evidence."

Leary smiled.

"I did, didn't I? I've kept your little secret as promised. That will still be the case if you agree to help me find the crosses."

"And if we don't?" asked Shannon.

"Well, you see. I still have a copy of that tape. I kept it for safekeeping, just in case there would be a time I needed it, and this is the time."

"You lying bastard!" shouted Shannon.

"Unfortunately for you, I'm not lying. The tape has been transferred to DVD. Very good quality. Digitally remastered. You both look great on it. Very distinguishable, even after all these years. Imagine if your bosses who sponsored this dig got a copy. What would that do for your careers and reputation?"

"You're bluffing," said Thomas.

"Isn't one of your bosses Anna Sweeney?" replied Leary.

"How do you know her?" asked Shannon, her voice almost a whisper.

"Well, she worked at Trinity with me in the library for some years in records. Always in the vaults and archives. That's probably why you didn't see her. We go way back and once had an intimate relationship. We still keep in touch and are very good friends. I'm sure she would be interested in my little story and film show."

"You bastard! What is it you want from us?" asked Thomas.

"Like I said, your help," replied Dermot.

Thomas regarded the older man.

"Why should I trust you? I obviously made that mistake before. I thought you were our friend."

"Wake up, boy. We could be onto a fortune here. You could be cut in. Can you trust me? Who knows? Can I trust you after what I told you? Let's work together and discover exactly what Declan Byrne discovered. Let's see if the legend is true. Do you honestly want the treasure to end up in a fucking museum and all you get is your name on a small display card next to it? I think you want this treasure as much as me, so do we have a deal?"

Thomas went silent. He knew that they had no choice. He also knew that he wanted those crosses.

They would have to go along with this arrangement. For now.

He looked up at Leary.

"Look, I'll level with you now. Since Professor Byrne let us into his secret, we've been trying to find the treasure ourselves. You're right. We're fed up with making discoveries for others to profit from and items ending up in some dusty museum."

It was Dermot's turn to smile now.

"So, will you help me??"

"50-50 split on the spoils?" asked Shannon.

Dermot inwardly thought *in your dreams*, but replied.

"Yeah. Why not?"

"And the DVD back."

Leary smiled.

"You got it."

Suddenly, they heard a car engine. Shannon stuck her head out of the tent to see who it was.

"Shit, it's the Garda!" she exclaimed.

Chapter 14

Sergeant Michael Drury pulled his considerable frame out of the squad car and walked towards the tent. The super seven fry-up and two mugs of tea he had consumed half an hour ago at Ginny's Roadside Food Truck sat uncomfortably in his stomach. He stifled a burp as he walked closer.

Thomas and Shannon suddenly appeared.

"My, my, Sergeant Drury. We're honoured to have your presence here. Did you get lost?" said Thomas with sarcasm dripping from his every word.

"Alright, lad. Watch your tongue now. I'm here on official police business."

From inside the tent, Dermot Leary listened closely.

"What is it?" asked Shannon.

"Down the road in a little layby is a badly burnt-out car. A Volvo, I think. Hard to tell as it's totally gutted out. You wouldn't know anything about it or heard anything in the last 24 hours?"

"I'm sorry, Sergeant, but no. We have no idea how it came to be in the layby or why it's burnt out. Was there anybody in it?" asked Thomas.

"Fortunately, no," replied the policeman.

He then looked about the site.

"Anybody else here that I could ask?"

"No. We came up early to the site. Nobody else will be here until around 9.00am."

"Right. Well, when they arrive, just ask them about the car and ring me if somebody knows anything."

"Will do, Sergeant."

Drury made to walk off, but then stopped and turned back.

"Any more trouble with nighthawks since we last spoke?"

Thomas shook his head.

"No, it's been quiet."

"There you go. I told you it would all peter out when they realised that they weren't going to find a hidden hoard of religious treasures. Load of old rubbish and superstition if you ask me."

Thomas and Shannon smiled.

"Maybe you're right after all, Sergeant."

Drury nodded.

"Right, I'll be on my way then."

"Oh, Sergeant, how's the drugs search going if you don't mind me asking?" said Shannon.

"I don't know, to be frank. A DCI Box took over the proceedings in the last few days. I have little involvement at present," replied Drury rather awkwardly.

They watched as Drury pulled his bulk back into the car and took what seemed like an age to put his seatbelt on and then start his engine and pull away.

Thomas and Shannon went back into the tent.

"I suppose you heard all that?" asked Thomas to Dermot.

"Aye, I did."

"Do you know anything about the burnt-out car?" queried Shannon.

"No, I don't. Some stupid joyriders probably nicked a car, had their fun in it and then torched it. Anyway, I suggest you put the kettle on, and we plan our next move. The inscription on the chalice leads me to believe the crosses are in a cave close to the abbey. I have with me a map of the area and coastline. Shall we take a look?"

* * *

Joe Regan pulled his 4x4 up outside the gates of the Clover Leaf Golf Club at 12.45pm. He got out and pressed the intercom on the wall. A female voice answered.

"Yes. How may I help?"

"My name is Joe Regan. I have a 1.00pm lunch date with Bertie Neil."

There was a moment's silence. Then, the voice spoke again.

"Okay, Mr Regan. When the gates open, just drive on up to the clubhouse. Mr Neil will meet you out the front."

Joe thanked the woman and returned to his vehicle.

The gates slowly and silently opened, and Joe drove on up the long driveway of the impressive hotel and clubhouse. Trees and shrubs lined the driveway in a very regal manner and the hotel and clubhouse stood out in all their glory up ahead.

As he pulled into a parking space, he saw Bertie walk out onto the steps leading down from the entrance of the clubhouse. He looked very dapper, dressed in a light blue suit, pure white shirt and navy tie. Joe felt a little underdressed in his brown Fat Face shirt, cream chinos and brown Timberland boots.

Bertie met him as he got out of his vehicle.

"Joe, how good to see you."

Joe shook the offered hand.

"And you, Bertie. This place looks the business."

"Let's eat lunch first and then I'll give you the tour and show you some of the antiques that are up for the auction."

"Great," replied Joe.

"It's such a lovely day I thought we would dine *al fresco* on the patio overlooking the green."

Joe followed Bertie up the steps and into the cool interior of the club. The reception area was huge, all marble and polished wood. Already Joe's antiques antenna had spotted some wonderful pieces.

A couple of John Boyne watercolours on the wall to the left caught his eye. Boyne was a famous Irish eighteenth-century painter, engraver and caricaturist.

In front of Joe was a beautiful coffee table by eighteenth-century furniture maker George Hepplewhite.

On the way out of the large open patio doors, Joe spied a sideboard with a dozen Meissen porcelain figurines of various animals. The craftmanship was quite stunning.

The place was, as Bertie mentioned, just like a museum.

Joe felt the heat of excitement that he always experienced when he knew that he was on the trail of real antiques.

Outside a young waitress showed them to a shaded table with a prime view over the golf course.

"What will you drink, Joe? Will you join me in a glass of chilled wine? We have a lovely Chablis Cru Les Bougros."

"Why not?" replied Joe.

He had a basic knowledge of wine, but underneath it all, he was a beer man.

Bertie regarded the young waitress. His eyes roamed all over her. Joe took this in and remembered the real reason that he was here to see this slimeball, but he also had to pick his moment carefully, especially in these surroundings.

"Natalie, sweetheart, bring us a bottle of the Chablis Cru Les Bougros, will you?"

The girl nodded.

"Yes, Mr Neil."

Bertie watched her walk away.

Joe opened his menu.

"Any recommendations, Bertie?"

The club captain brought his attention back to Joe.

"Well, the wine would be a great accompaniment to the breadcrumbed crab cakes and brown rice."

"Sounds a perfect choice for a summer's day. I'll go with that."

Bertie seemed pleased with himself.

"Excellent."

The wine soon arrived, and Bertie did the honours of pouring it.

Both men sampled the ice-cold floral flavours.

"Good choice, Bertie," said Joe.

They clicked glasses.

"So sorry to hear Maggie couldn't make it," said Bertie.

Joe felt a flicker of adrenaline in his belly. He pushed it down.

"Well, she knew I would probably end up talking shop and bore her, so she's better off at home. She'll probably go to the woods and do some sketching by the lake. You mentioned the lake the other day. Do you know the area there well, Bertie?"

Bertie took a measured sip of wine.

"You know what? I haven't been out there in an age. I used to swim in the lake, but it must be a couple of years since I've done that. Of course, I know the cottage, but I haven't really explored beyond that in some while."

"Oh, is that so? It really is beautiful there," replied Joe.

Bertie swiftly changed the subject.

"Do you miss the police force, Joe?"

Joe's eyebrows rose quizzically.

Bertie saw this and quickly added.

"Maggie mentioned it to me when we ran into each other yesterday."

"Oh yes. She did mention that," replied Joe, watching Bertie like a hawk, "Well, in answer to your question, yes, sometimes. When I watch the news or read about some scumbag perpetrating a heinous crime, I do get the urge to hunt the bastard down and put him away. I really was quite good at it in my time. I still find it difficult to accept that I'm not a copper. I have a habit of sticking my nose in business I should really stay clear of. I'm working on it though."

Bertie laughed nervously.

"I've read online about you. You have an impressive background."

"Checking me out, eh?"

Bertie smiled.

"Yes. Something like that. Just curious really."

"Yeah. Well, like I say, that's all in the past now. These days I try to just deal in antiques, and I'm looking forward to what you have to show me."

The lunch arrived and the men made small talk over it as they enjoyed the wonderful food. Joe stuck to the one glass of wine, but Bertie finished off the bottle. He wanted to keep a clear head. Plus, he had to drive.

After lunch, they enjoyed a coffee before Bertie gave Joe the full tour of the club. The whole place reeked of money and privilege. The room that Bertie brought Joe into to show him the sellable antiques was like an Aladdin's cave.

"Look, I'll leave you for a while to browse around. No pressure."

When Bertie left, Joe moved about the room taking photos on his phone. He knew that he would have buyers for a good few items, so he wanted to get as much detail as possible.

Two rare standout items were a beautiful cranberry coloured Whitefriars vase worth a few grand and an unusual Troika lamp by Penny Black worth around £1,800. He had two collectors who would be drooling over these.

When Bertie returned, Joe gave him a list of what he could sell and the prices he thought that they would fetch at auction and at a private sale.

Bertie looked suitable impressed and informed him that he would have to speak with the club's chairman, Julian Finchley, in the next day or so and then get back to him, but he did not foresee any problems.

"Now, let me show you the club's hidden gem," announced Bertie.

"Sounds intriguing."

"It is, but it's not an antique as such."

Joe followed Bertie down past the green to the cliffs where they came to an ornate wrought iron gate. A sign on it read *Fairy Cove.*

Bertie punched a code in on a keypad and opened the gate.

"For an extra fee, our guests have exclusive access to this private beach and cove. They can swim, sunbath, dine or party in complete privacy. Nobody can use it, apart from our lucky members who have the money for that extra special occasion."

Both men walked down a winding set of stone steps carved into the cliff. Halfway down was a beautiful stone balcony built into the cliffs with a sunroof.

"The tides can be unpredictable here, so were built this balcony area for people to eat, chill and enjoy the view if the tide is in or the weather is poor. After all, this is Ireland and not Tenerife."

Bertie continued.

"It's named Fairy Cove after the little folk who were said to live here and who supposedly guarded a horde of gold somewhere in the cliffs. Ireland loves its myths and legends. It all adds to the flavour of the experience, I suppose."

Both men now found themselves on a beautifully secluded and private sandy beach.

"The cove is tidal, unfortunately, but with have a top-class weatherman and ex-sailor on the committee, they work all that out for us. The tides come and go quite quickly along this stretch of coastline, so we get plenty of use out of the beach, weather permitting, of course."

Along each end of the cove were high wire fences shutting it off from any public. Large buoys bobbed along in the water, forming a straight line like an army guarding the shore. They cordoned off the area. No boat could sail into the shallows.

To the right against the cliff face was a large billboard, advertising that the cove was private property of the Clover Leaf. Intruders will be prosecuted.

"Do you get many people trying to access the beach without permission?" asked Joe.

"No, not really. The coastguard patrols the area regularly, so it would be difficult to try," replied Bertie, "Besides, there are plenty of other coves and beaches along the coast for recreation."

The deep blue sea looked inviting in the afternoon sunlight.

"How long has the club owned this stretch of beach?" asked Joe.

"Well, as far as I know, it came with the land the club and hotel was built on. It was one of those agreements that go back decades and decades. The club has been here 20 years now and it's always been ours," said Bertie, "Before that, I think it was open to anybody."

"Wow, this is some place, Bertie," exclaimed Joe, "I'm impressed. I bet it impresses the ladies as well. Am I right?"

Bertie, feeling chilled on the alcohol he had consumed at lunch, laughed.

"Well, Joe. I have used this place on more than one occasion as... how shall I put it?"

A sickly grin spread over his face.

"As foreplay. It certainly has the desired effect, I can tell you."

Joe smiled back.

"I have a feeling you're a bit of a ladies' man, Bertie."

"It has been known. I'm a sucker for a lovely face or a nice pair of legs."

Joe laughed and then moved up close to Bertie. His voice carried menace when he spoke.

"Just so that we have no misunderstandings here, Bertie, let me make something clear to you. When it comes to your womanising, Maggie is off limits. Understand?"

Bertie looked shocked, but Joe could see guilt on his face.

"Of course, Joe. I don't understand. Has Maggie said something to you? I can assure you, I have done nothing inappropriate."

"So, why were you were creeping around the lake behind the cottage spying on Maggie?"

Bertie again looked surprised, but quickly composed himself.

"That's not true. You have no proof of that."

"Is that right?" said Joe, "When you so graciously gave Maggie a lift home last night, she found a receipt in your blue windbreaker for an ice cream from the van in the park beyond the lake with yesterday's date and time on it. It proves beyond doubt you were in the vicinity. You told me earlier you hadn't been to the lake in years. That was a lie."

"What the hell was she going through my pockets for? That jacket is private property."

"Because you unnerved her yesterday and she isn't a woman to be scared easily," replied Joe, "You're a liar, Bertie. You were at that lake sculking around."

Joe now got right up in Bertie's face.

"Weren't you?"

"Fuck you, Joe."

Bertie went to swing a punch, but it was far too telegraphed. Joe brought his knee up into the man's balls and Bertie dropped to the sand. Joe stood back, knowing Bertie was not going to be a threat anymore and waited until he recovered.

Bertie's shoulders slumped in resignation.

"Okay, yes, I was at the lake, but not to spy on Maggie. I didn't realise she would be there. It's not what you think."

"So, enlighten me then," said Joe.

Bertie sighed again.

"The receipt Maggie found did come from the ice cream van by the lake, but if she had looked more closely, she would have seen it was for an ice cream and an ice lolly."

Bertie hesitated.

"I met a woman there. She's married to the golf club treasurer. We've been having a clandestine affair for a few months. We try to be discreet in where we rendezvous. Yesterday I was meeting her, not stalking Maggie. I did see Maggie briefly when I was coming back to the lake, but I made myself scarce so that I didn't have to explain why I was there. I panicked, Joe. Now, in retrospect, I should have made my presence known."

"Yes, you should have. You frightened her unnecessarily and caused her distress."

Bertie raised his hands.

"I'm truly sorry, Joe. I didn't mean any harm. Look, I know I can be a bit of a dick sometimes, but I truly didn't mean to creep her out. What can I do to make it up to you and Maggie?"

Joe was quiet for a moment.

"I should make you give me a few of those antiques on my list for nothing, but my past policing conscience will not let me do that."

Bertie laughed nervously.

"I have a better solution. I had a couple today have to cancel their spot on the beach tomorrow evening. How about you and Maggie come and use it? On the house, of course. Friday evening from 7.00pm through to midnight. Food and drink included. What do you say?"

"Well, that is very generous of you, Bertie. We'll take you up on that offer. We plan to move onto Cork on Saturday morning, so that would be a perfect send-off."

"Okay, Joe. You've got it. Are we straight then?" asked Bertie.

"Yes, we're straight."

"And my little secret remains that way?"

Joe sighed.

"Yes, Bertie. I'm not interested in your love life. Just stay away from Maggie, okay?"

Bertie nodded.

"Shall we go back up?" he said.

Joe smiled and headed back up the steps.

Bertie winced as he followed.

Chapter 15

Dermot Leary stood at the cliffside beyond the abbey, looking through a pair of binoculars. He studied the surrounding cliffs intensely.

Earlier over a mug of tea with a splash of whiskey added, Thomas Cahill, Shannon Brady and Leary had all studied the journal and the chalice. They all had come to the same conclusion that the crosses were hidden in a cliffside cave very close by. All they needed to do was now discover it.

Leary had asked the pair if they had ever heard of the little chapel, but both of them told him no. He believed them.

All the information they had at their disposal suggested that the crosses were real after all, just not yet discovered.

As others arrived at the dig, Thomas and Shannon went to meet them and give out instructions. Shannon also rang Jerry Dooley's phone again, but with no reply. She left a text message asking him to contact her as soon as he received the message. It was odd that he was not here on site as he had been first there every day and keen to help.

Meanwhile, Dermot had gone back to his car, got hold of his binoculars and made his way to the headland to scrutinise the cliffs. He felt that he needed a boat to approach the cliffs from the sea to have a better chance of finding a cave of any sorts. It must be well hidden. Otherwise, fishermen or tourists would have discovered it well before now.

Heading back to Thomas, he asked if he knew any local boatman who might take them out around the coast. Thomas told him that he knew a man in Carrickburn who had a 22-foot Boston Whaler recreational fishing boat. The man was a local named Andy Sharkey. Thomas had done a bit of fishing and snorkelling from his boat in the past when he was in the area.

"Is he trustworthy? The sort of man who would turn a blind eye and ask no questions for a nice little earner?" asked Dermot.

"He is sound. I have heard that he did a bit of bird years back. Receiving stolen goods, I believe. Andy seems solid enough. A boatman around here will take any work he is given in this economic crisis."

Dermot thought how ironic it was that he was slipping further and further into the criminal fraternity. He wondered what his old grey colleagues at Trinity would think of that.

They would not understand the sheer excitement of the hunt for these treasures, nor would they understand why Dermot was going to sell them for a great deal of lifechanging money and not donate them to a stuffy museum. Well, fuck them and their vanilla lives. They had all looked through him when he worked at Trinity. He was about to have the last laugh on the stuck-up bastards.

"Have you a number for him?" he asked Thomas.

The younger man pulled out his phone.

"I'll find it on his webpage."

"Right, lad. Get him on the phone and see when he can take us out and what it'll cost. Tell him the trip around the cliffs are to tie up with your dig. You won't be far wrong. Just don't tell him what it is you're looking for."

Thomas nodded, pulled out his phone and walked away a short distance to make the call.

Dermot continued to scour the cliffs. He could see off to his left where the golf club was situated, but it was quite obscured from here. Beyond, he saw the black and white of Fergal Rock Lighthouse. To his right, the cliffs jutted out and also impeded any sight to the further coves up the coast. The boat was the only way that they would find this cave.

Thomas came back.

"Well?" asked Leary.

"He can take us out tomorrow at 7.00am sharp for a couple of hours, but then he's booked up the rest of the day with clients. 150 cash. I took the liberty of telling him yes. I know where he's moored up in Carrickburn Harbour."

"Good," replied Dermot.

Shannon walked up and they filled her in on the plans. She seemed happy with them.

Dermot then said.

"I'm staying at the Ferryboat Inn in Carrickburn. Why not join me for dinner tonight?"

"Well, we're staying in Carrickburn too, so that would work out alright. Then, we'll both be there for the morning," replied Thomas.

"Excellent," said Dermot, "Shall we say 7.30pm in the bar?"

"Great," replied Thomas.

"We all good now?" the older man asked, "We've come to a mutual understanding. Yes?"

Thomas nodded.

"We're all good."

The younger couple watched Dermot Leary walk away towards his car.

"Do you trust him?" asked Shannon.

Thomas smiled ruefully.

"About as much as a fat boy in a doughnut shop. No, he'll try and screw us. We have just got to be smarter than him. If we have dinner with him tonight, at least we know where the slippery bastard is. I suspect he's thinking the same where we're concerned."

"Right," acknowledged Shannon.

As they walked back into the main tent, they noticed that the chalice and journal were both gone from the tabletop. A scribbled note read:

Just took them both for safekeeping in case the police come snooping around again. Dermot.

Shannon regarded Thomas.

"What did you just say about us having to be smarter?"

Thomas shook his head in disbelief.

"Don't worry. He won't do anything with them. For now, he needs our help locating the crosses."

Thomas crossed to the kettle.

"Fancy a cuppa?"

"Why not," answered Shannon, "Oh, by the way, I phoned Jerry twice more with no reply. Neither has he left a text. Do you think he's alright?"

Thomas shook the kettle, then plugged it in and flicked the switch.

"I think big Jerry can look after himself. Anyway, we don't need him anymore, seeing the chalice has been unearthed. Probably better he isn't around."

"And Joe Regan?"

"Just a tourist passing through, I think. I don't think we need to worry about him any further. All we have to do is keep an eye on Dermot Leary."

"Do you believe his story about Byrne giving him the journal for safekeeping?" asked Shannon.

"No, I don't," answered Thomas, "I think he knows more about the professor's death than he's letting on."

Suddenly, Shannon looked frightened.

"Is he a danger to us?"

"I don't think he actually murdered Byrne. More likely he paid somebody else to do it or it was just an accident. Don't get me wrong. He's ruthless and I am by no means a fighter, but I think I can take care of Leary if he tries something. Also, Andy Sharkey is a fucking handful if things kick off. I think we'll be quite safe and soon we're going to be rich."

Shannon came into his arms and kissed him passionately. Her hands moved down to his crotch suggestively.

"Hey, what about the tea? The kettle has just boiled," said Thomas.

Shannon smiled seductively.

"It can wait, Big Boy. It can wait."

* * *

Joe arrived back at the cottage around 4.30pm. Maggie was not about. He rang her mobile, but it went to answerphone. He was mildly concerned after what had happened, but he did not want to be overprotective of her.

After the incident with the killer, Brendan Quinn, Joe had made sure that Maggie was always safe, but he knew that he could not be there for her all the time and nor would she want him to be.

It was just her recent encounter with Bertie that had put him at unease, although that issue seemed now to be cleared up. He could not wait to tell her about Bertie giving them use of the private beach.

He waited another ten minutes and tried Maggie's phone yet again without success.

He decided to walk down into the woods and find the lake. She was probably still sketching. *But why then hadn't she answered her phone when she saw it was me calling?*

Joe walked towards the back gate. As he did, he tried Maggie's phone once more. It went to answerphone. He now picked up his pace.

Joe walked through the woodland path. The trees gave him a canopy of shade from the late afternoon sun, but he found that he was still sweating. The path seemed to go on forever and every step that he took found him more anxious.

He took a deep breath and tried to rationalise things and come up with possible reasons why Maggie was not answering her phone. Being an ex-copper, he could not help the fact that his mind always came around to the worst-case scenario. Finally, he came to a clearing and, up ahead, saw the lake. As he walked nearer, he saw Maggie's sketchpad and shoulder bag, along with her sandals and a half-drunk bottle of water. But no Maggie.

He scanned the lake and then he saw her floating in the middle of the water spreadeagled. His heart skipped a beat. With panic in his voice, he yelled out her name.

"Maggie!"

Maggie sprung upright in the water and looked to the shore. Her face lit up into that wonderful smile and she waved at him.

"Hi, Joe. What a lovely surprise."

Joe felt the tension flow out of his body and his taut muscles relax.

Thank God. For one horrible moment...

Joe now glanced down and saw her phone tucked in one of her sandals.

Maggie swam to the shore and walked out the water. She was wearing her red swimsuit and looked stunning.

"It's glorious in there. So cool. The weather has been a scorcher today, so I decided to bring my costume and take a dip."

Joe tried to sound light-hearted and chilled.

"I tried phoning you a couple of times when I got back home with no reply, so I thought I would come and find you."

"I'm sorry, Joe. I must have been swimming and never heard it. I hope I didn't cause you concern. I'm perfectly alright. I knew you were with Bertie, so I felt safe."

Joe smiled.

"It's fine, as long as you're okay.

Maggie came up to Joe. They embraced and kissed. Her body was wet and cool. Joe liked the sensation that he felt.

"If I had known you were swimming, I would have brought my trunks."

Maggie nibbled his ear and then said seductively.

"Who needs trunks, Buster?"

Joe laughed.

"Maggie Scott, what on earth are you suggesting?"

Just then, they heard laughter and a couple of youngsters on bikes appeared from the woodland path, along with a blonde-haired woman.

"Can we go swimming, Mummy? Can we?" they both echoed.

The blonde-haired woman, who looked somewhat flustered, said.

"Yes, you can, but give Mummy five minutes to sort out your swimming things, okay?"

Joe smiled at Maggie.

"I think we'll give the skinny-dipping a miss today."

"Oh, what a shame," replied Maggie.

She reached into her bag, pulled out a purple sarong, tied it around herself and slipped on her sandals. Joe helped her gather up her belongings and they headed off back home arm in arm.

"How did it go with Bertie then?" asked Maggie.

"Very well actually. We got things sorted out."

"Really?"

Maggie studied Joe's face.

"And he's alright, is he?"

"Of course. In fact, he was very apologetic and as a gesture of goodwill, he had given us exclusive use of the club's private beach cove for a champagne dinner on Friday evening."

"Are you kidding?" answered Maggie.

"No, it's all true. We have the place from 7.00pm through to midnight if we want it."

"Wow. He did this voluntarily?"

"Yes," replied Joe, "I think the poor chap was mortified with what he did. He's harmless really."

"What about the jacket and receipt?" asked Maggie.

Joe put his arm around Maggie.

"I'll tell you all about that, but you're sworn to total secrecy."

"Now I'm intrigued," replied Maggie.

* * *

A little later, the cottage came into view.

Maggie was still amazed at the deal that Joe had sprung with Bertie. What a treat. She was also relieved to find out that Bertie may be a womaniser, but not some mad stalker.

As they walked through the garden and around to the front of the house, they saw a man stood at the gate looking towards the outhouse. Joe thought that he looked vaguely familiar. He was an imposing sight. 6'4" at least and around 114kg. He had a shock of grey hair and matching beard. Maggie thought that he looked like a stereotypical Viking warrior.

"Can I help you?" asked Joe.

The man looked momentarily startled by their sudden appearance, but he quickly pulled himself together.

"Sorry, I didn't mean to intrude. I used to know the old fella that owned the place, Desmond Coyne. I did some work for him on the cottage and the outhouse. I was just passing and thought that I'd take a quick peep at the old place. I miss him. He was a great character."

"Oh, I see. Well, I'm Joe and this is Maggie. We're renting it for a short while. You're welcome to take a look around. We're just about to have a coffee if you'd like one?"

"No. That's very kind of you, but I have to be on my way. Sorry for any inconvenience. Just reminiscing."

Joe smiled.

"No problem. We all tend to do that as we get older. I didn't catch your name."

'Oh right. Jerry Dooley."

Joe then knew where he had seen the man before.

"You are up at the dig in the abbey, aren't you? We were up there the other day. I thought you looked familiar. I never forget a face. Part of being an ex-copper, I suspect."

Jerry's face could not hide his surprise.

"Yes. I was helping on the dig for a while. Anyway, like I said, I must dash. Nice to speak to you."

With that, the big man headed across the road to a rusty white van, jumped in and was gone.

"Something I said?" asked Joe.

Maggie laughed.

"Some people have a weird reaction when you mention you used to be in the police force."

Joe looked on down the road where the van had disappeared.

"Mmm. Maybe. But in my experience, they only react like that when they have something to hide."

Maggie grabbed his hand and pulled him towards the cottage.

"Come on, Lieutenant Columbo. Let's get that coffee. Shall we?"

* * *

As Jerry drove, his mind was in turmoil. What was the chances of a fucking ex-policeman renting the cottage? Would this guy go rooting about the place and find the bag? There was just too much at stake. He had one more day to wait before he was due to collect it and hand it over. Could he afford to sit it out and wait?

The thought required a drink, so he pulled in at The Speckled Cow and ordered a large Jameson's while he mulled over the problem at hand.

He finally calmed down and thought rationally. He decided to leave the bag where it was. Copper or no copper, this guy had no reason while he was on holiday to be rooting about in the dusty eaves of the outhouse.

Jerry realised that he had panicked. Things were getting tense as it came down to the wire. He had never seen Noel Best so edgy. This was a very important deal and it had to go smoothly for everybody's sake.

All would be fine. He just had to keep his nerve. He would go back in the early hours of Saturday and retrieve it.

He then thought back to the three men that he had encountered at the dig sight the other night. It still riled him that the older man had escaped him, but he was sure that he had only been interested in that gold chalice. He would have surely heard about it if he had gone to the Garda. He felt that he was safe on that score, but the sooner he got out of Ireland, the better. Noel Best could find another monkey to do his dirty work.

Where would Jerry head? He decided that this question needed some contemplation with the help of another Jameson's.

* * *

Later that night, Joe lay in bed looking at the ceiling and going over today's events. Somewhere nearby, he could hear the hooting of owls. They sounded close. He had heard them most nights. They were definitely not in the woods. He felt that they were somewhere closer.

Today had been a strange mixture of emotions. The confrontation with Bertie. The panic when he couldn't find Maggie and then a strange feeling about this Jerry Dooley staring at the property.

Joe had no real reason to feel suspicious about the man, yet he felt a sense of unease. The holiday break to Ireland had been a memorable experience, but there had also been many unexplained questions over the death of Declan Byrne. Was there a connection between his death and the dig at the abbey?

He knew that he would be moving onto Cork in a few days and then back home. Joe had no direct involvement in the case, yet he still felt some sense of responsibility towards Byrne. He wanted to help, but had no idea how.

Maybe he should just let it go. But this had been Joe's problem when he was policing: he could not let anything go. His sense of commitment and quest for justice had been second to none. Joe's dogged persistence and never say die attitude had helped him solve a record number of cases, some which had lain cold for years.

But that was the past. Right?

He had Maggie now and Hidden Treasures, his shop back in Oakcombe.

But was it enough?

Suddenly, he heard a noise in the back garden. He slipped out of bed, went through to the spare room and looked out the window.

At first, he could see nothing, but as a cloud moved away from the moon, the silvery glow lit up the garden. Joe saw a fox sniffing around the recycling boxes. He smiled to himself and went back to bed.

It took a while before sleep eventually came.

Chapter 16

Dermot Leary, Thomas Cahill and Shannon Brady all waited at the harbourside at Carrickburn while Andy Sharkey prepared his vessel. The air was chilly, but at least the weather was still fine. It was 7.25pm. The man had turned up late and smelling of whiskey. Not a great start.

Sharkey was in his late 40s, bald and built like a pitbull, but he seemed affable enough.

"Nearly ready. Then, we'll crack on. Got the money, have you?"

Dermot nodded.

"Yes, I have it."

"Good. Right we are then. Come on then. Hop aboard."

Andy Sharkey extended a hand to guide Shannon on board, but let the two men find their own way on.

"So, we'll head out towards the old abbey and the lighthouse, is that right?" he asked.

"Yes, that's right," replied Thomas, "As I said, we're part of the dig up at the abbey. We're also involved in the possibility of finding a sea cave along that stretch that the monks used as a chapel. It would be an amazing find if we could prove that."

He hoped his story sounded convincing enough to Sharkey, but the man did not seem too bothered.

"Like I said, I need to be back by late morning. Until then, I'm all yours."

He looked to Dermot.

"I'll have the fee up front if you don't mind."

He stretched a calloused hand forward and waited for Dermot to place the agreed 150€ in it. Sharkey quickly counted it and put it in his pocket, smiling to himself.

"Okay. Let's cast off."

With that, he untied the rope holding the boat in place, started the engine and away they went.

The day was overcast, but pleasant enough. No rain was forecast.

The three sat at the rear of the boat. The waters were pretty calm with very little swells. Shannon was grateful for that as she was not a great sailor and preferred her feet on *terra firma*.

All three of them were excited at the prospect of discovering the cave and what might lie within. The night before after dinner at the Ferryboat Inn, they had taken their drinks to a quiet corner of the bar and studied a map of the coastline. They all agreed that the cave would be close to the abbey, so they homed in on that area.

There were three major coves near the abbey. All of them were only accessible from the sea unless you were a good abseiler and climber.

Fairy Cove by the golf club. Smugglers Cove near the lighthouse. And Drummond Cove further around the bend from the abbey.

They all agreed from Declan Byrne's journal that it was one of these.

The problem was that the coves were tidal, so for a good part of the time, they were underwater.

Much of the coastline had a semi-diurnal tide, meaning that it had two highs and two lows each day, with minimal variation in the height of successive high or low waters. This could make the sea caves hard to spot, but luckily this morning the tide was going out, so they had a good chance of spotting them if they were there.

It took them about 25 minutes to reach Drummond Cove. The beach was visible, but there were no apparent cave entrances in the cliffside.

"Is it worth getting off?" asked Thomas.

Dermot's keen eyes roamed over the cove. He then used his binoculars.

"No. I don't see any openings. Let's move on."

The boat now made its way to Fairy Cove. It could only get so close because a line of buoys prevented any vessel pulling into the private beach. There were private beach signs everywhere and the large billboard informing intruders that the cove was owned by the golf club.

"I think they want to keep out the riffraff," said Dermot.

This early in the morning, though, there was nobody about. Again, Dermot brought the binoculars to his eyes and scanned the cliff. A lot of rocks had fallen in that area. Could an opening be obscured? There were also a lot of bushes, growing out of the cliffside making it difficult to ascertain if a cave existed there.

"Well?" asked Shannon.

"Not sure. Too difficult to tell from here," replied Dermot.

"So, what shall we do?"

Dermot paused for a moment, then spoke.

"Well, Shannon, I think before we get wet, we should check out Smugglers Cove first."

They all agreed.

It was a ten-minute journey to the cove, but it proved fruitless.

"As I expected. This one is probably too far away from the abbey. Let's go back to Fairy Cove."

As the boat made its return journey, another small cove came into view with a sandy beach and a small rowing boat laid up there.

"What about there?" asked Thomas.

"I don't think so," replied Dermot, "Still too far away."

"What is that cove called?" enquired Shannon.

Dermot consulted his map. He had to study it hard to find it.

"Ah, here we go. Breaker Cove. There's nothing near it. According to the journal, it's the only cove in the area that you can get direct access to from a pathway. The public walk down there regularly, so I'm sure a cave would have been mentioned. I believe the pathway leads back up to the main road where you'll find a few holiday cottages. It just doesn't feel right."

"Yes, you're right. That's where that ex-cop is staying at present up in one of those cottages," said Shannon.

Dermot Leary became concerned.

"Ex-cop? What do you mean?"

"He came up to the site at the abbey a few days back. He said he was on holiday. He's an antiques dealer now, according to him. I looked him up on the net. DCI Joe Regan, Scotland Yard. He's highly decorated and a bit of a hero by all accounts. He said he was also a friend of the professor."

Dermot paled.

"Have you seen him since?"

"No," replied Thomas, "I believe it's a coincidence he's here. I'm sure he's nothing to worry about."

Dermot took the information on board. He felt slightly uneasy, but had to push on ahead. He had come too far.

The boat sailed back to Fairy Cove.

"Right. Now, listen up," said Sharkey, "As soon as you put foot on that beach, you'll be trespassing on private property. That's your business, but if the coastguard comes down here sniffing around, then I'm off and you'll have to fend for yourselves. You understand?"

"Yes, we understand," replied Dermot.

The three passengers then got out into the surf and waded waist deep to the beach. They kept their eyes peeled for any sign of people from the club or hotel.

Andy Sharkey moored up by one of the buoys and decided to brew himself some coffee while the others went ashore. All the time he kept a sharp eye out.

The cove was beautiful and, obviously, the golf club looked after it. It was immaculately clean.

Walking over to the cliff wall, the three looked behind fallen rocks and stone and pushed away bush and bracken, looking for anything that resembled a cave.

Fifteen minutes passed with no success. Then, Shannon called out.

"Quickly! Over here! I think I've found something."

The two men quickly joined her by the large billboard.

"Look here. Behind the billboard. I think I've found something. There's some sort of opening here in the rocks. It's not very wide, but it may lead to more."

Dermot pushed forward and shone his torch into the opening. He gasped as he saw the inside. It was a passageway leading into the cliff itself.

"Well, what do you think?" asked Thomas.

Dermot could not contain his excitement.

"I think we're onto something, but we need to explore further."

"Right. Well, let's do that," urged the younger man.

"No. Wait!" replied Dermot, "We need somebody to stand guard here and keep an eye out and also make sure Sharkey doesn't maroon us here."

"Okay. Shannon can do that."

"No, you need to do this, Thomas. We need a male presence. Shannon can come with me."

Thomas looked apprehensively at Shannon.

"Will you be okay?"

"I'll be fine," she said.

"We won't be long. This is just a reccy to see how far the tunnel goes. If it goes on and on, we'll need to come back with proper equipment to go further into the cave. Okay?" said Dermot.

Thomas nodded.

"How long will you be gone?"

Dermot looked at his watch.

"I make it 8.30am. We'll be about 20 minutes. Okay?"

* * *

Dermot and Shannon switched on their torches and squeezed through the aperture. It was narrow and dark inside, but after a few minutes, the passageway began to widen.

The sand was damp underfoot and there were puddles everywhere. They tread carefully as the ground was also littered with stones and seaweed, as well as bones of small animals.

The air was damp and salty.

As they shone their torches forward, the passageway went on and then bent off to the right. They both carried on around the bend and the tunnel continued on an upward slope deeper into the cliffside.

After ten minutes of walking, they came to a dead end where rocks and stones had fallen, but there was a very small opening uncovered.

Dermot tried to shine his torch in there, but with little success. The darkness beyond was almost impenetrable.

"We'll have to come back with tools to remove this rubble, but I'm confident this tunnel goes on beyond here. I truly believe we're on to something. Declan Byrne was right."

They began to make their way back along the tunnel.

Dermot looked at Shannon. She had a sheen of sweat on her forehead and she looked pale.

"You okay?" he asked.

Shannon nodded.

"Yes, I'm fine. I think I may be coming down with a cold."

She quickly changed the subject.

"When do we come back? This being a private beach, how on earth can we dig here without being seen?"

"We'll have to do it at night. That's the only way."

"Will Sharkey bring us out here at night? Won't he think it strange? Also, what about the coastguard coming back and forward?"

Dermot smiled ruefully.

"If we cross his palm with silver, so to speak, I think Sharkey will do as he is told and keep an eye on a possible visit from the coastguard."

When they both reappeared from the cave, Thomas was waiting there anxiously.

"How did it go?"

Shannon filled him in on what they had found.

"I think we've found it. It makes sense. I heard Sharkey mention on the way over that this cove, like all the others along here, are tidal. That means between the water and the billboard up on the cliff, the cave entrance has been obscured for years. Nobody from the sea would know it was there. Plus, the beach being private to golf club members for partying only, there would be no beachcombers exploring the surroundings."

"It makes sense," said Thomas.

"I agree," stated Leary, "If the good monks did hide those crosses in there, then they were exceptionally clever. That opening would have been totally unseen from the water."

They decided to head back to shore and discuss their next course of action. The three had begun to form an uneasy alliance.

Once on the boat, Andy Sharkey pulled away quickly.

"Find what you were looking for?" he asked.

Dermot looked at the other two sternly and then answered cagily.

"Not sure really. We'll need more time there to explore."

"Why not ask the golf club if you can work at the cove. If it's part of an authorised dig, they can't object," suggested Sharkey.

Dermot knew what Sharkey said was feasible, but he also knew that if the golf club got involved and found out that they had discovered something on their property, they would want a piece of it. He could not let that happen. He already had the problem of the two with him on the boat. When their use ran out, he would have to find a way of getting rid of them.

He did not want anybody else involved. Too many had died already. He had blood on his hands, but he had experienced blood on his hands when he had been in the army. He knew that he would do whatever was necessary to find these crosses.

"Yes, I could ask the golf club, but I want to be sure first before I involve them," he answered.

Andy smirked across at the three of them.

"You must think I'm stupid."

"What do you mean?" asked Thomas.

"There's something hidden in that cave. Something valuable. If there is, I want in on it or I go to the golf club myself or maybe to the bosses of your dig."

Sharkey had a glint of menace in his eyes.

"Are you trying to blackmail us?" asked Leary.

"Damn right I am. I want in or I talk."

Dermot thought quickly. He needed to stop this situation escalating.

"You saw right through us, Andy. Sorry to treat you like a fool. We believe there may be treasure left by smugglers back in the day. The tunnel leads through the cliff. We think some of the treasure is still in the cave somewhere."

"What sort of treasure?" asked Sharkey.

"Coins, we think."

Sharkey took this information in and then spoke.

"So, what is your next move?"

"I'm not sure," replied Leary warily, "I'll have to chat with my colleagues. I have your number, so I'll call you tomorrow. Okay?"

"You better do, mister, or I'm singing like a bird to all the right people. Understand?"

Leary nodded.

"Yes, Sharkey. You've made yourself clear. If we find this treasure, there will be more than enough to cut you in."

This seemed to satisfy the man.

Dermot looked at the other two and imperceptibly shook his head to silence them.

Once off the boat, the three made their way to the Ferryboat Inn and ordered coffee.

"What are we going to do about him?" asked Thomas.

"It was you who said he was sound, remember?" replied Dermot.

Shannon cut in.

"And it was you, Dermot, who said he would do anything for a few quid. Obviously, you were both wrong and underestimated him. He wants a damn sight more and he's not the sort of person you say no to by the looks of it."

"Okay. I need time to think. You get back to the dig. The others will begin to wonder where you are. I'll contact you later."

"Are we still going to meet this man tomorrow night?" asked Shannon.

"At this moment in time, I don't see that we have any other choice."

* * *

After Thomas and Shannon left, Dermot Leary walked back down to the harbourside. He watched as Sharkey's boat *The Princess* set off with a small group of fishing clients. The owner of the boat next door called up to Dermot.

"Looking to go out, are you?"

Dermot regarded the grizzly features of a 'Captain Birdseye' lookalike.

"Well, I was due out with Andy, but it looks like he forgot me," he lied.

The old man laughed.

"No surprise there. Sharkey is a walking distillery. Can't find his ass with both hands. I'm surprised he can sail at all."

Dermot laughed.

"Likes a drink, does he?"

"He's a pisshead. Never sober. You're better off going out with me than trust that lunatic."

Dermot watched *The Princess* disappearing out of the harbour.

"I'll bear that in mind. Thank you."

As he walked off, a plan began to formulate in his mind.

Chapter 17

When Thomas and Shannon got back to the dig site, they saw Annie Shaw, the volunteer they left in charge, talking to what looked like two plain-clothed policemen. Annie was a bit of a fusser, and she was looking a little flustered. When she saw the two of them, she waved them over rather franticly.

"Everything okay here?" asked Thomas as he got closer.

"Thomas, Shannon, this is the Garda. They would like a word. I was trying to help them, but I don't really know what to say."

"Okay, Annie. Thank you. You can go back to your work," said Thomas.

The policeman regarded them both. He then glanced at his notebook.

"You're the dig supervisors, Thomas Cahill and Shannon Brady?"

"That's correct," answered Thomas.

"I am DCI Ryder, and this is WPC Hewson."

"How can we help you? Is it about the burnt-out car again?" asked Shannon.

The policeman seemed confused.

"No. That's being looked into by somebody else."

He consulted his notebook again.

"I believe you knew a Professor Declan Byrne, recently deceased?"

Thomas felt a tingle of adrenaline in his belly.

"Yes, we did know him. He was our university lecturer and mentor at Trinity College."

"He was also thinking of helping out with funding some of the dig here. Is that right?" asked Ryder.

Thomas glanced at Shannon and then quickly turned back towards the policeman. The exchange had not gone unnoticed by Ryder.

"May I ask why he wanted to help fund the dig?"

Thomas knew that he had to tread carefully when he answered. Obviously, the police had cottoned on to something which brought them here.

"The dig was winding down, but the professor – being a fanatic of Gaelic history and a leader in his field – felt more time should be given to unearthing the abbey's secrets, so he told us he would help us out financially with a donation."

WPC Hewson was now taking notes.

"In a desk diary of the professor, he had written a note that he planned to come and visit the site, but with no specific date given. Did he get here?" asked Ryder.

"No," replied Thomas, "Unfortunately, he never did."

Ryder nodded.

"I see."

He looked around the site, deep in thought, and then asked another question.

"Do you know why he was coming here? From his medical records, he was not a well man and didn't leave the house very often. It must have been something special to get him to come here from his home in Dalkey."

Thomas swallowed hard.

"As I said, the professor was passionate about his work, but he didn't disclose to us why he was coming here. He just said that he would tell us when he arrived."

Ryder then changed tack.

"We believe his death was the result of a break-in being disturbed, although nothing seemed to be taken. However, his housekeeper has mentioned she believes that a journal is missing. One that the professor had been particularly close to."

Ryder stared Thomas and Shannon in the eyes.

"Do you know anything about a journal? Did the professor ever mention it to you?"

Thomas held his gaze steadily.

"No, I'm afraid we don't know anything about it. Isn't that right, Shannon?"

Shannon nodded.

"That's right."

She then asked innocently.

"Is it important, this journal?"

Ryder regarded them both.

"Maybe. We're yet to find out. But if it's gone missing, then there has to be something within it worth stealing for and indeed taking a man's life. Are you sure he never mentioned it?"

Thomas shook his head.

"As I already said, no. He never did. It's tragic what happened to the professor. He was a dear friend and inspiration, but we can't help you anymore than we already have."

Ryder seemed satisfied.

"Do you know a man named Dermot Leary? He was a good friend of the professor.

Thomas shook his head.

"Can't say I have. Is he involved in some way?"

Ryder regarded him.

"Let's just say he's a person of interest at the moment. Anyway, thank you both for your time. I may be back if anything develops."

"We'll be here and only too willing to help if we can," answered Thomas.

Ryder made to walk away and then turned back.

"Oh, by the way, Sergeant Drury mentioned something about you having trouble with nighthawks. Is that still going on?"

Thomas smiled.

"No. They seemed to get fed up when they realised there was nothing of value here to steal."

Ryder looked about the place again.

"I have known about this place since I was a lad. There were always rumours of buried treasure here."

Shannon laughed.

"So everybody tells us. Well, if you call a few plates, cups, coins and arrowheads treasure, you're in the right place."

It was Ryder's turn to laugh.

"Not going to be in the press with the next big archaeological find then?"

"Not on this site," answered Thomas.

"Oh well. I'll be on my way."

Ryder then paused.

"Funny though."

"How do you mean?" asked Thomas.

"Well, if this dig is such a washout, it's funny why the professor would want to pour money into it. Maybe he knew something you didn't. Maybe he wrote it in down in that journal of his."

Thomas and Shannon said nothing.

Ryder smiled.

"Sorry, just thinking out loud. Anyway, I won't keep you any longer. Good day to you both."

With that, both police officers got into their car and drove off.

* * *

Thomas and Shannon watched the car disappear and then they went into their tent.

"What do you make of that?" asked Shannon.

Thomas sat down into a chair and run his hands through his hair.

"Well, obviously, they are onto the journal, but Leary has it and the chalice. There's nothing to tie us to either, so I don't think we have anything to worry about at this stage."

"Why don't we just shop Leary to the police and have done with this?" said Shannon.

Thomas got up from the chair, went to her and gripped her shoulders tightly. He looked her in the eye.

"No. We can't give up now. We're close. This find is the only way we're going to get to America and find a cure for you. You know the clock is ticking. We can't wait any longer. I don't want to lose you, Shannon."

His voice cracked and tears formed in his eyes.

They hugged each other.

Six months ago, Shannon had been diagnosed with the rare disease, chronic myeloid leukaemia, after having felt tired and listless for some time. She was immediately put on the medicine Imatinib designed to slow down the cancer, but it was not a cure.

Chronic myeloid leukaemia was a steady and deliberating illness. It brought about a genetic mutation in the stem cells, which caused a huge overproduction of white blood cells and a corresponding drop in red blood cells and platelets. This lack of red blood cells caused symptoms of anaemia, such as tiredness, while the lack of platelets increased the risk of excessive bleeding.

In the USA, there was pioneering bone marrow and stem cell treatment, which may reverse the process or delay progression at the very least. However, before transplantation can take place, the person receiving the transplant would have to undertake aggressive, high-dose chemotherapy and radiotherapy to destroy any cancerous cells in their body.

This would put enormous strain on the body and could cause significant side effects and potential complications. Due to these issues, transplantations were usually only successful when they were carried out in children and young people, or older people in good health, and if there was a suitable brother or sister who could provide a donation.

Thomas and Shannon thought that it was worth the risk. However, the price for this treatment was astronomical. Their only hope was to find and sell these crosses to pay for the lifesaving treatment.

"Hold your nerve and we'll get what we want. Just don't give up, Shannon. Promise me."

Shannon smiled through her tears.

"Okay, Thomas, but I'm scared."

"So am, I but we must be brave."

"What about Leary? You know he isn't going to share the spoils if we find these crosses."

Thomas kissed Shannon on the forehead.

"Leave that to me to worry about. Now, come on. We'd better do some work."

Chapter 18

WPC Emma Hewson looked at the notice on the shop door and tried the handle hopefully. She looked back to the car parked at the kerb side in which sat DCI Keith Ryder.

"All shut up, Gov. Looks like this Dermot Leary might be on his holidays."

"Shit," mouthed Ryder.

From the dig site, they had driven all the way to Dublin to speak with this Dermot Leary. It had taken the best part of the day to get here and now he was not about.

Their investigation was hitting dead ends at every turn. This Leary character, according to Eileen Fergus the housekeeper, had been a really good friend of Declan Byrne and may have been the last person to have seen him alive apart from her. They needed to contact him.

It seemed strange that he went away on holiday when the professor was dead. Wouldn't he want to help? Or maybe he had gone away before the murder? If he was away somewhere like Thailand or Australia, for example, he would not know anything about it, would he?

Leary was not a suspect, just an interesting connection to Byrne at this present moment. At this stage, they did not want to push looking for Leary any more than need be.

They had obtained Leary's mobile phone number, but it appeared to be switched off. If he was in foreign parts, he would be hard to trace. Hopefully, he would return home soon. If this did not happen in the next few days, then Ryder would consider obtaining information from his phone provider under the Investigatory Powers Act. Then, if the phone was still switched off, the police could employ triangulation or GPS to track it.

Hopefully, it would not come to this. If this Dermot Leary was as close a friend as Eileen Fergus said and he did not know about Byrne's death, he was going to be in for a hell of a shock when he found out.

They also had not located the missing journal or indeed had any word on it. Maybe Leary could shed some light onto what exactly was written in the journal?

Ryder looked towards WPC Hewson.

"Okay, Emma. Let's knock on a few doors nearby just in case he left any contact details with a friend."

They both began to knock on doors near to the shop, including the flat next door, but with little success.

A neighbour who did answer, a Mrs Rose Touhey, told the police that Leary was a private man who kept himself to himself. She did mention, however, that he had two rottweiler dogs, which she had not heard barking recently. Ryder and Hewson thanked her.

"Maybe Leary put them in dog kennels until he returned," said Hewson.

"Yeah, maybe," replied Ryder.

As they both stood outside Leary's flat once again looking up at the bedroom windows, Patrick Malone, who had been out walking Leary's dogs and coming to check on the shop, came around the corner. He spied the two people and instantly knew that they were Garda.

He should know as, for many years in his younger days, he had been a petty thief and burglar. He had, therefore, got to spot a copper pretty quickly. That was all in his past now, but he still did not like talking to him.

Before either of them spotted him, he turned heel and headed back in the direction he had come from. He wondered what the police were doing at Leary's place.

He did not know Dermot Leary well. They had only become friendly when Patrick, who was now a painter and decorator, spruced up the lounge and kitchen in Leary's flat with a good lick of paint. They had got talking and hit it off well. Since then, they had met up a few times at the pub around the corner, The Shilling, for a few drinks and a hand of cards.

The other day, Leary had unexpectedly called him and told Patrick that he had an emergency to attend to and would it be possible for him to look after his dogs? It had put Patrick on the spot, but he liked Dermot, so he had agreed.

The bottle of malt whiskey Dermot had left him had been a nice touch too. What he did know of Dermot Leary in the brief time they had met was that he a lovely old guy and seemed harmless enough. He was puzzled as to why the police were knocking on the door of his flat.

* * *

Dermot Leary opened his suitcase and lifted out an object wrapped in a hand towel. He placed the object on the bed and uncovered it. He stared it.

It was a gun. A World War Two Webley Mk VI six-round revolver. It had been his father's, who passed it onto him when he died.

Dermot treasured the piece and cleaned and maintained it regularly. He was also a terrific shot from being a champion marksman when he had been in the forces.

He snapped open the chamber and checked the bullets. They were all there. He closed it again, wrapped it up and returned it to his suitcase.

This was the equaliser he needed to obtain the crosses for himself. Sharkey would not be so tough when he was staring down the barrel of that baby. No, sir. The man would do whatever Leary wanted. Thomas and Shannon would also shit themselves when their time arrived.

He now unwrapped the chalice and once more admired its beauty. How much it was worth was anybody's guess, but it was going to be big bucks when he offloaded it.

Leary now picked up the journal and flicked through it. It had served its purpose and had brought them to the cave at Fairy Cove where Leary was in no doubt the crosses were situated.

He contemplated now disposing of the journal. It was not really needed, but something compelled him to hang onto it. In a way, it was a provenance to the treasures and may add a few more quid to the pot.

Ten minutes ago, he had received a phone call on his burner phone from Patrick Malone, informing him that the Garda had been knocking on the doors of his shop and flat and also speaking to the neighbours.

Leary realised that he could not stay incognito forever. The police would be suspicious about why his phone was switched off. Sooner or later, he would have to speak to them to allay any of their suspicions. He would tell them that he had had his phone stolen and had not had the time to get a new one as yet. That might work.

But first, he needed to find the crosses.

* * *

Joe Regan sat in the garden reading a paperback book. The book was entitled *Picture You Dead* by his favourite crime author, Peter James. He had read all his stuff and especially enjoyed the DCI Roy Grace novels. This latest one was right up his street as it was a murder mystery set in the antiques world. Perfect.

Maggie was sat close by sketching the gateway and path leading to the woods. It was 2.00pm on another sunny afternoon.

They both sipped contentedly on G&Ts, enjoying the peace and solitude. They were looking forward to later today when they would go to the beach at the golf club. What a perfect way to finish off this leg of their Irish road trip.

Earlier that morning, Joe had been up at the crack of dawn again finding it difficult to sleep. He had gone for a run along the cliffs and ended up at the abbey. He had not intended this. He had just ended up there.

It was only 7.30am by the time he got there, so there was nobody around. On impulse, he had decided to take a walk around the site, being careful where he tread and not to touch anything.

All was quiet and serene, except for the sound of the sea lapping the shore. As he looked around, it seemed that they had excavated a fair bit of the area. He wondered what had been discovered. He also wondered exactly what it was that Declan Bryne had been so sure was buried here.

Thomas Cahill had said that Byrne believed real buried treasure was here and he knew exactly where to look. Was that why he was murdered? Did somebody else find out his secret? Did that somebody steal the journal to help them find a buried horde? And if so, how would they uncover it with the dig going on?

Joe's mind was turning over and over the events of the past week.

Did this Dermot Leary hold the clue? If so, where was he and why hadn't the police found him? Did Thomas and Shannon know more than they were letting on?

Back in his day, he would have been back here questioning them more thoroughly, and he would have found Leary too.

He knew DCI Ryder was a good copper and that he should leave him to it, but he felt that the local police were more wrapped up in finding the drugs stash than finding out the murderer of the professor.

Should he call Ryder with his suspicions?

But what did he really have?

Nothing concrete. Just that gut feeling that a copper never loses.

***

Jerry Dooley had been lying low since his encounter with the ex-cop up at the cottage where he had hidden the drugs. He was staying in a flat of a friend who was away on holiday.

Jerry had decided to move out of Carrickburn for the moment. The flat was up the coast a little bit in a small fishing village called Portkearn. It was quiet there and people kept themselves to themselves. Just how Dooley wanted it for now.

The time was nearly here. In the early hours of tomorrow morning, he would retrieve the drugs and drop them off to the Ink Man.

Jerry was sat in the kitchen of the flat, sipping on a mug of coffee and reading the local paper. He came across the latest update about the murder of that professor who had been linked to the dig at the abbey. Up to now, he had not really given it much thought, but what sparked his interest was the information released by the Garda about a missing journal belonging to the professor. They believed whatever was in the journal was the reason for the man being murdered.

This information brought him back to the three men digging that night on the site. He also now remembered the book he found lying in the grass after clearing up the site and disposing of the two younger men's bodies.

It certainly matched the description of this missing journal. He recalled it full of scribbles, diagrams and other writings he could not make head nor tail of.

He was now convinced that he had stumbled across the missing journal, and he figured that the three men digging there had been using it. Had he inadvertently crossed paths with this Professor Byrne's killers?

He mulled this fact over and concluded that he probably had. It had been a complete coincidence that they had dug up the bag of drugs. What were the chances?

Dooley wondered what the secret in the journal had been and had the lone man found it? He knew that he would never find out the answer as he was not planning on staying in Ireland after tomorrow. However, he did allow himself a wry grin when he thought about the absurdity of the situation that night at the dig.

If they had murdered this Declan Byrne, two of them had paid the price for it.

Dooley also realised how lucky he had been to get away with the murders of the two men and how nothing had come back on him. Still, he realised the sooner he was out of the country, the better.

* * *

Dermot Leary watched Andy Sharkey walk into the Ferryboat Inn at around 8.00pm. The man was already a little worse for wear after spending an hour or so beforehand in The Golden Anchor.

Leary had been discreetly watching the man for some while now. Sharkey was drinking whiskey and it was going down like water.

He had left a few friends at The Golden Anchor and was now on his own as he ordered a double Bushmills at the bar of the Ferryboat Inn. As Sharkey reached in his pocket for his money, he heard a voice next to him say.

"I'll buy that, and give me a single as well, please."

Through blurry eyes, Sharkey recognised Leary.

"Well, well, well, if it isn't the treasure hunter. Thanks for the drink."

Leary smiled.

"You're welcome. Have you a minute to talk?"

Sharkey took a gulp of his drink.

"Talk away. I'm in no hurry."

Leary gestured to an empty table in the corner.

"Shall we?"

Sharkey grabbed his drink and walked unsteadily over towards it. Once both men sat down, Sharkey leant in close to Leary.

"Well, what can I do for you? Or should I ask what you are going to do for me?"

"Well, that's why I'm here. After today, I'm convinced that we've found the right location of the treasure, but seeing as the beach is private, I need to get on there at night. And that's where you come in."

Sharkey smiled drunkenly.

"You want me to ferry you out there in the dead of night and trespass on that beach?"

Leary took a small sip of his whiskey.

"That's about the size of it, yes."

Sharkey swallowed the remainder of his drink.

"Well, that's a mighty big risk to take. It'll cost you big if I take it on."

Leary took the man's glass and stood up.

"Maybe another drink will help you decide, eh?"

Another hour and a few more whiskeys, Sharkey was up for the adventure.

Leary had excused himself to the toilets for five minutes and had called Thomas Cahill telling him and Shannon to meet him down by Sharkey's boat at 11.00pm. He told them to bring flashlights and shovels.

When he returned from the toilets, he stood Sharkey another double. By the time they left the pub and headed to the boat, Leary was practically holding Sharkey up.

* * *

The night was perfect for Joe and Maggie's date at the cove. The forecast threatened storms later, but in the early evening sunshine, that seemed unlikely.

A table had been set up on the balcony and waiter service had been provided. Before dinner, Joe and Maggie had enjoyed a few champagne cocktails sat looking out to sea.

Dinner had been a starter of crab pâté on toast, followed by a main of succulent sea bass and a dessert of raspberry tart and vanilla ice cream. The meal had been cleared away and they now sat on two plush loungers sipping brandy and watching the sunset in a magnificent array of golds and red. A fire burned brightly in a fire pit below. It was all quite idyllic.

"I could get used to this," said Maggie.

Joe stretched back on his lounger and smiled.

"Yep. So could I."

"That meal was delicious, and the surroundings are to die for. Bertie certainly kept his promise. I feel a little guilty now. Maybe I misjudged him," mused Maggie.

"No. You had him sussed. He certainly sees himself as a bit of a lady's man, does our Bertie. Hopefully, it did him some good to be put in his place, although I somehow doubt it."

"Well, I'm just glad he's not about. I don't really want to see him," replied Maggie.

Joe topped up his glass from the bottle of Courvoisier Imperial cognac, which tasted like nectar and was slipping down rather too easily.

"He's entertaining a party of visiting Japanese golfers this evening. I think you'll be safe. We have the code to the gate when we're finished. We just damp down the fire, switch off the ground lights and go back up the stairs and head home. We don't even have to go back into the golf club or hotel as there'll be the same car waiting which brought us here to chauffeur us back home."

"That is music to my ears. Now, top up my drink and then give me a kiss," said Maggie.

"Yes, madame. On my way," replied Joe.

Chapter 19

The Princess made its way out onto the dark waters. As drunk as Sharkey was, he probably could have made his way to Fairy Cove in his sleep as he had taken his boat out in that direction countless times.

Leary watched him steer the boat surprisingly smoothly out of the harbour and then off to the cliffs beyond.

Thomas and Shannon sat at the back of the boat quietly. Both their stomachs were knotted with fear and anticipation of what the night would bring. They were excited about the pending discovery, but worried about what Leary would do once they found the crosses. He did not seem the sharing type.

Both of them were also now convinced that he had something to do with the death of Declan Byrne, which made this man unpredictable and dangerous. Thomas had to be ready for him when the time came. He was not a fighter, but the six-inch hunting knife that he had concealed in the rear waistband of his jeans gave him some degree of comfort.

"So, when we get to the cove. I will stop where I did yesterday and you get to the beach," said Sharkey.

He studied his watch, taking time to focus his gaze on it.

"It's now 11.30pm. You'll have roughly an hour and a half before the tide starts coming into the cove, so you better be ready by then or I'll leave you all to fucking drown."

Sharkey laughed cruelly.

Leary nodded.

"We'll be ready."

Sharkey looked towards Leary.

"Don't even think of trying to fuck me over when you find these coins. Understand?"

"I have no guarantees we will find them in the time allocated," replied Leary.

Sharkey grinned drunkenly.

"Then, you'll have to work fast, won't you?"

He looked down on the deck to where Leary had placed a tool bag.

"You'd better use those tools wisely."

Sharkey turned back to the wheel as the cliffs loomed closer. Just around the next bend would be the cove.

Leary now took his chance.

"Oh, I will use them wisely. You can bet on that."

Reaching down into the tool bag, he picked out a lump hammer. To the horror of Thomas and Shannon, they watched him swing it with considerable force down onto Sharkey's skull. The noise it made was sickening.

Sharkey sunk to his knees. Pain exploded in his head, and he could see nothing but black dots before his eyes. He tried to stand, but another blow put him down and out. Breathing heavily, Leary looked towards the stunned couple at the back of the boat.

"Give me a hand. Quick."

Neither of them moved. They just stared at the fallen body of Sharkey.

Leary stood with the bloodied hammer still in his grip and shouted angrily.

"You, boy! Get up here now and help me."

Thomas slowly got to his feet.

Shannon gripped his arm and whispered.

"Be careful."

Thomas walked towards Leary, never taking his eyes off the hammer.

"Right. Grab his legs and I'll get his arms."

Leary put the hammer down.

Both men struggled to lift the dead weight of Sharkey, but eventually hoisted him level with the side of the boat.

"Right. On the count of three," said Leary, "One, two, three."

They rolled the body overboard and it crashed into the dark sea. The bloodied hammer followed.

Leary now took control of the boat. He had some basic knowledge of sailing from his younger days. His father had owned a little 12-footer and Leary had fished off it on many occasions as a lad. He was confident that he could sail the boat near to the cove and then back home later.

"Right, that takes care of that blackmailing bastard. Now the treasure is all ours."

"Fuck, Leary! You just killed a man! Do you not care?" said Thomas.

Leary turned on him.

"Listen to me, boy. That man wanted to take a share of the treasures and I couldn't let that happen. Men like him would keep coming back for more. Plus, he was a drunk who wouldn't be able to keep his mouth shut. He was a fucking liability. Think about it."

Thomas sat back down with Shannon and gingerly felt for the knife in his waistband. It was still there.

For now, he knew that they were both safe as Leary needed their help in the cave. It was later that he was worried about. Leary had disposed of Sharkey like a garbage bag and had shown no remorse.

* * *

Joe poured a bucket of water onto the fire and switched off the ground lights. They both were tidying up any rubbish before leaving when suddenly a light cut through the darkness.

"It's a boat coming in close to the cove," said Joe.

"Is it to do with the golf club?" asked Maggie.

"I don't know, but as far as I knew, no boats were allowed into this area," replied Joe.

Maggie looked out to the sea and then back to Joe.

"Maybe we should go up and tell somebody," she suggested.

Joe drew her close to him.

"Let's just wait a minute and see what's going on."

They huddled down behind a small outcrop of rocks and watched as a boat pulled into the swallow waters and stopped. Three people waded across onto the beach. They were carrying shovels, rucksacks and what looked like tool bags. They all wore headtorches.

"A bit late for beachcombing, don't you think?" whispered Joe.

Maggie said nothing, but Joe felt her grip on him tighten.

As the three figures came onto the beach, the clouds shifted, and the moon momentarily lit everything up in an eerie glow.

Joe recognised the young couple from the abbey dig site. There was also an older man with them whose face looked familiar, but Joe could not place it at that moment. The three of them disappeared behind the large billboard by the cliff and did not reappear.

What was going on here?

"Let's go, Joe. I don't know what's going on, but I don't feel good about it," said Maggie.

"Maggie, I want you to go up to the club and tell any member of the staff that there are intruders on the beach," instructed Joe.

"What are you going to do?"

"I'm going to stay here and keep watch."

Maggie looked at Joe.

"Promise me you won't do anything heroic."

Joe smiled.

"I promise. Now, go get the cavalry."

Maggie kissed him and disappeared up the steps from the beach.

When she had gone, Joe suddenly remembered who the older man was. The face in the photograph with Declan Byrne. It was the elusive Dermot Leary. He was sure of it.

Now, what were those three doing together down here in the dead of night?

* * *

Dermot, Thomas and Shannon had made it back to where the rocks had blocked the passageway.

"Right, let's start shifting these," said Leary.

The three began the task of moving the rocks from the opening. Luckily, none of the rocks that had fallen were large or heavy; it was just a tedious job of moving them away from the aperture. They used the shovels and their hands.

"Don't forget the time," said Thomas, "Remember the tide."

They worked quickly and made good progress.

After half an hour or so, there was an opening big enough to shine a torch through. With trembling hands, Leary shone a torch into the darkness. As his eyes became adjusted to the light, he gasped in disbelief.

"What is it?" asked Shannon.

Leary swallowed hard.

"My God, Declan was right! The old bugger was right!"

"What do you see? For Christ's sake, Leary, tell us!" pleaded Thomas.

Leary turned towards the expectant faces of the young couple.

"The crosses. They're sat on what looks like a stone altar. They're just sat there as if waiting to be discovered. It's unbelievable that they've been here all this time untouched."

Thomas moved up to the hole and pushed his face close to it, so his headlight illuminated the black beyond.

Leary was right. Sweet Jesus. The 12 Celtic crosses did exist. The legend was true.

He turned back to Leary and Shannon.

"We need to get to them before the sea takes them, as the inscription on the chalice foretold. The rock fall here has protected them and ironically stopped them being washed away."

The three now frantically moved more rocks and shovelled away stones, increasing the opening little by little.

* * *

Joe heard footsteps coming down the steps and looked up to see Bertie and Maggie. Unfortunately for Maggie, Bertie had been the first person that she had seen in the reception, and he had immediately approached her. Any awkwardness between them was forgotten for the moment, however. They joined Joe on the beach.

"What's going on, Joe? I just ran into Maggie in the foyer looking really distressed. She told me there are intruders on the beach here."

As he said this, he looked around furtively.

Joe pointed.

"They sailed in on that boat and then disappeared over there and have not come back. My guess is that there's a cave or an opening behind there," answered Joe.

"But why? Nothing like this has happened before," said Bertie.

"That's what we need to find out," replied Joe.

Bertie looked at him as if he had gone mad.

"Now, hang on a minute, Joe. I suggest we contact the police and let them deal with it."

"I agree," said Maggie.

"Okay. Maggie, go up to the hotel and get them to contact the police. Bertie and I will stand watch, won't we?"

Bertie, whose face was deathly pale, nodded.

Maggie looked at Joe. She had got to know this man inside and out. The good and the bad.

"Joe, I swear to God if you go looking for these people, I will personally kill you myself."

Joe gently grabbed her shoulders.

"I promise I won't go in there. Now, hurry."

Maggie disappeared back up the steps.

"What the hell do you think they're looking for?" asked Bertie.

Joe told Bertie about the dig at the abbey, the missing journal and Declan Byrne's staunch belief of hidden treasure somewhere nearby. He also stated that he recognised the three people.

"You think they've uncovered some ancient horde?"

"Yes, maybe they have."

Bertie looked at Joe, a small gleam appearing in his eye.

"Well, if that's the case, it's on the golf club and hotel's property, so it technically belongs to us. Plus, they're also trespassing on private property."

Joe nodded.

Bertie suddenly sounded braver.

"I'm going to take a closer look."

Joe reached out to stop him, but the man was walking briskly towards the cliffs.

"Wait up!" called Joe.

* * *

"That's it," exclaimed Dermot Leary, "That's big enough."

They stood back and looked at the gap they had uncovered.

"Right, in you go. Let's get those crosses."

Thomas and Shannon clambered into the opening, just as Leary had instructed. The surroundings were a small cavern with a stone altar. On top, laid out in a line, stood proudly the twelve Celtic crosses.

The couple were in awe. They had read so many stories about these legendary relics, but never truly believed that they existed. And now, here they stood. A massive slice of ancient history and, in monetary terms, priceless. For a moment in time, they were seduced by the find.

Leary threw a canvas bag through the opening.

"Here. Put them into this. Hurry!"

As he spoke, he felt dampness around his feet and looked down to see the water seeping into the cave. The tide was coming in.

Thomas and Shannon began gathering up the crosses and putting them into the bag.

"Right, hand it out to me!" instructed Leary.

This was the moment. It was now or never. Thomas reached behind him, pulled out the hunting knife and brandished it.

"Fuck you, Leary. Step back out of the way and don't try to stop us or I swear to God, I'll kill you. You murdered Professor Byrne for these crosses and Sharkey. You've also blackmailed us, but now you get your comeuppance."

Leary looked at Thomas and burst into laughter.

Thomas and Shannon could not understand why.

"Don't laugh at me, Leary. I'm serious."

Leary's laughter died out after echoing around the cave.

"Oh, I'm certain you are serious. After all, you want the treasure for yourselves as well, don't you? Don't act holier than thou with me, you bastard."

Thomas nodded.

"Yes, we want the treasure, but for better reasons then you. Yours is just pure greed."

"And yours?" asked Leary.

Thomas glanced at Shannon.

"She is ill and needs special treatment in the States. It's the only hope that she'll survive. I've now concluded if I hand over the crosses to the authorities as the sole finder, the reward will be enough for that operation to happen. The money means nothing to me without Shannon."

Leary smiled.

"How touching."

He reached into his coat pocket and produced the revolver.

"Drop the knife, boy, and you, Shannon, hand me out the bag."

Thomas and Shannon froze as they saw the gun.

Leary pointed it at Shannon, but spoke to Thomas.

"You're right. I am responsible for two deaths, maybe in a roundabout way even more. So, you will believe me if I tell you that your girlfriend dies if you don't do as I ask."

As Leary spoke, he felt the sea water now up to his ankles.

"Quickly. The tide is coming in. Give me it now!"

Leary cocked the trigger and fired a shot into the rock next to Shannon. She screamed and flinched back in terror.

"You bastard!" shouted Thomas.

He lunged towards Leary with the hunting knife.

* * *

Joe and Bertie heard what sounded like a gunshot. They both looked at each other.

"Look. Maybe we should wait for the police after all," said Bertie, his eyes wide with fright.

"I can't," said Joe, "It sounds like somebody is in trouble. I have to help."

With that, Joe disappeared behind the hoarding and soon found the cave opening. He reached into his coat pocket for his car keys. On the end of them was a small but very bright LED torch. He snapped it on and walked forward into the darkness, suddenly aware of water rushing around his ankles. As he swiftly moved forward, he heard another gunshot echo and vibrate through the cave.

* * *

Thomas fell to the ground, clutching his left side. Shannon screamed and dropped the bag, rushing to his aid. Leary reached in and picked up the bag. Shannon looked at him with hatred in her eyes.

"You bastard. You didn't need to do that. He needs medical treatment. He's bleeding heavily."

"Tough," replied Leary, "He should have done what I asked. Anyway, it doesn't matter. The tide will be in here soon and it'll be all over for the both of you. You'll never be able to make it out in time."

Shannon knew that his words were true. She had not told Thomas, but all the exertion of moving the rocks and stones had left her feeling badly fatigued and weak. She would never be able to help him get out on her own. Panic ensued her.

"Please help us. Take the crosses. I don't care. Just get us out. We won't tell anybody what has gone on here. Please help us."

Leary looked at the water, which was now knee deep. He then looked Shannon in the eye.

"Even if I wanted to, it's far too late. The sea is going to fill this cave very soon. I have barely time myself to escape."

"Wait, Leary. In that case, please do one last thing. Shoot us both. Don't let us drown in this cave. Just put us out of our misery."

Leary stared at her pleading face. He levelled the gun.

"Okay. As you wish."

Suddenly, he was hit from behind by a hard rugby tackle. He pitched face forward into the water and his gun disappeared from his hand and so did the bag.

Leary scrambled over onto his back, but Joe Regan maintained his position on top of him. Joe swung a left hook, connecting with Leary's jaw. It landed perfectly, knocking the man out.

He now got to his feet and looked towards Thomas and Shannon.

"Come on. I'll help you out."

"It's Thomas. He's been shot. He's lost a lot of blood."

"Okay," said Joe, "I'll get him. What the hell are you doing in here?"

"It's a long story and we haven't got time to discuss it now."

"Yeah, of course," replied Joe, eyeing the rising water.

As he walked forward, he heard a noise behind him and spun around to see Leary coming at him. In his right hand was the hunting knife that Thomas had dropped when shot.

Leary lunged the blade in a stabbing motion towards Joe's abdomen. Joe was instantly transported back to that night many years ago when he was attacked on his doorstep by crazed criminal Eddie Keen. He had been stabbed multiple times. His body still bore the scars. Every day he looked in the mirror reminded him of the horror.

That night, he had somehow managed to survive and take Keen out, but it had ultimately ended his career. The incident had haunted Joe for many years. In all truth, it had never fully gone away, although he had learned to cope with it. Now, it all came rushing back.

Joe moved back from the blade and kicked out low at Leary's knees, trying to keep him at bay. Leary came forward again, slashing the knife in a frenzy. Joe once again backed off and kicked out, but this time, the slippery floor of the cave became his undoing and he fell backwards. He swallowed a mouthful of salty sea water before winding himself on the rocks underneath him.

Leary grinned triumphantly and raised the knife in an ice pick grip, ready to administer the killing blow. Suddenly, he froze in place as a heavy rock connected with his skull. He dropped the knife and fell unconscious to the floor.

Joe looked up through his pain to see Bertie standing there wide-eyed with a bloodied stone in his hand.

"Shit, Joe. Are you okay?"

At that moment in time, Joe could have kissed the bastard.

Suddenly, flashlights filled the cave and police descended upon them, as did the paramedics whom Bertie had called after hearing the gunshots.

"Right, we have no time to waste. Everybody needs to get out of here fast," said a burly police officer.

Joe got to his feet. He was wet and cold, but no worse for wear.

As the paramedics helped Thomas and Shannon out of the small inner cavern, Shannon grabbed Joe's arm and whispered.

"Over there by the wall. That bag. Please bring it. It will explain everything."

Chapter 20

The paramedics took Thomas straight to hospital and Shannon went with them. Before getting in the ambulance, she found Joe and asked him to give the bag over to the Garda.

Another ambulance whisked Dermot Leary away, who was still unconscious. A police guard accompanied him. They were desperate to speak to him as soon as he regained consciousness.

DCI Keith Ryder took brief statements from Joe, Bertie and Maggie once paramedics had checked them over.

Joe then handed the bag over to Ryder.

"Apparently, this is what they were looking for in the cave. The girl, Shannon Brady, asked me to give you it."

Ryder took the bag, placed it on a table in the front gardens of the golf club and unzipped it. He reached in and pulled out a cross.

"What the hell have we got here then?" he asked, "I was hoping it would be the stash of cocaine that's missing, not some old cross."

Joe's eyes glistened in the moonlight and his heart skipped a beat. He knew – or rather guessed – what they were.

"That one old cross, Keith, is worth more than your missing drugs. If there's another eleven in that bag, we've hit the jackpot."

Both men delved into the bag, producing more crosses.

"If I'm not mistaken…" said Joe, "… these are the twelve mythical crosses of St. Columba. Treasures that most said were legends, but I suspect not Professor Declan Byrne."

"Columba? What? That monk who said he saw the Loch Ness Monster?" exclaimed Ryder.

"The one and the same, Keith. I believe Byrne's stolen journal contained the whereabouts of the crosses and he was murdered for it and the unconscious man who tried to kill Thomas and Shannon is responsible."

Ryder nodded.

"Would that man be the elusive Dermot Leary?"

"I believe it is. Byrne's closest and most trusted friend. How ironic."

Maggie came up and wrapped her arms around Joe.

"Can we go home now? I've had enough excitement for one day."

Joe looked at Ryder.

"Yes, you can go home, but you'll have to stay around a few days so that we can get a full written statement from you both."

"Sure thing," said Joe.

As they turned to walk away, they spied Bertie sipping what looked like a brandy. He looked ashen and shaken up. Joe went up to him and extended his hand. Bertie took it and shook it.

"Bertie, I want to thank you for saving my ass. I truly thought I was a goner."

Bertie smiled weakly.

"I'm just glad I had the balls to come look for you and not run the other way. I'm not much of a hero, I'm afraid."

"You did good," replied Joe.

"Yes, thank you, Bertie. I truly mean that," said Maggie.

Bertie nodded shyly. He then coughed awkwardly.

"I couldn't help but overhear. What do you think will happen to these crosses?"

"Well, I suspect the police will hang onto them for evidence and then the proper authorities will get them. Some big museum, no doubt. It truly is the find of the century. It will be front page headlines all over the world."

Bertie was silent.

Joe punched his shoulder lightly.

"I also suspect the golf club will get a substantial award for them being found on their property and also a shedload of media coverage. After all, you are the hero of the moment."

Bertie smiled.

"I suppose you'll be off once the police have finished talking to you?"

"Yes," replied Maggie, "I think we've had enough drama and excitement for a while."

Joe laughed and put his arm around her.

"All the best, Bertie, and thanks again."

"You're welcome. Make sure you come back to visit soon."

"We will," said Joe.

Bertie gestured towards the driveway of the golf club.

"See the green Jaguar? The chauffeur there will give you a lift home."

"Amazing. Thank you," replied Joe.

In the back seat of the car with the privacy window up, Maggie looked at Joe.

"What happened to '*I will stay exactly here*,' Joe? You promised me."

Joe looked at her.

"Maggie, I swear I was going nowhere until I heard the gunshot and couldn't stand by when there was a chance somebody was hurt."

"That's all very admirable, but what about your safety? If it hadn't been for Bertie showing up, you may well be dead. It's not your job anymore to rush in where angels fear to tread."

Joe sighed.

"Point taken."

Maggie grabbed his hand.

"Is it though, Joe? You've said all that before, yet here we are again in another life and death situation. Some people have said that you have more lives than a cat, but I seriously think you've used them up."

"I'm sorry, Maggie. I never planned any of this or could have foreseen what was going to happen."

Tears came to Maggie's eyes.

"Joe, I love you, but I can't live this way. I feel the life you have with me is not enough. You still crave the action and excitement of your old life."

"That's not fair, Maggie. I love you more than anything. I want to spend my whole life with you."

"If that's the case, the way you're going, it's going to be a bloody short one," replied Maggie.

The rest of the journey was travelled in silence, both of them deep in thought.

* * *

At the hospital in Carrickburn where the paramedics had taken the casualties, Thomas Cahill was stable after his wound had been seen to. The bullet had gone right through him, fortunately missing any vital organs. His condition was described as comfortable.

Shannon was resting on a ward from exhaustion and shock, but apart from that, she was as well as expected in her condition.

Dermot Leary was still unconscious. The blow he had received to the head had been a heavy one. He was being monitored around the clock for any improvement.

DCI Ryder and WPC Emma Hewson were for now waiting in the hospital reception, trying to piece together what had happened.

The girl, Shannon, had told them that Leary had confessed to Thomas and her that he was instrumental in Professor Byrne's murder and the thief of his journal. She also told them Leary had murdered boatman Andrew Sharkey.

She went on to explain that Leary had blackmailed them into helping him unearth the crosses and they had been unwilling accomplices to what had transpired. Neither Thomas nor Shannon had any police record, so their story rang true for now.

Ryder had found a room key to number 20 of the Ferryboat Inn in Leary's inside jacket pocket. Sergeant Drury had been dispatched there immediately and, in a suitcase under the bed, he had found the missing journal and a golden chalice. Both were winging their way to Carrickburn Police Station.

The police who had been in the cave had also retrieved the revolver that Leary had used. The evidence was stacking up against the man.

The press was already beginning to sniff around after a big tip off from an anonymous phone caller. They sensed that they were on to something major. Apparently, they were already up at the Clover Field Golf Club, Hotel and Spa talking to Bertie Neal.

Murder, violence, hidden treasure. The stuff Agatha Christie would have been proud to have written about.

DCI Ryder knew that he would not be able to keep the media in the dark for very long. His superiors in Dublin were also demanding progress quickly. He hoped that Leary would come around soon, so that he could hear his side of the story. Hopefully, he could put the whole incident to bed soon.

"Coffee, Gov?" asked Hewson.

"Yes please. Black, two sugars. I have a feeling we've got a bit of a wait on our hands."

* * *

When Joe and Maggie got back to the cottage, it was 2.30pm. Maggie told Joe that she was going to bed.

"Can we not sort this out, Maggie?" asked Joe.

Maggie regarded him.

"It's too late now. Let's talk in the morning. Okay?"

Joe nodded.

"Okay, Maggie. I'm going to stay up for a while. I'm too wired for sleep."

Maggie gave him a weak smile.

"Don't be too long."

When Maggie had gone upstairs, Joe poured himself a generous measure of Jameson's. He switched all the lights out and flopped down onto the sofa in the darkness.

He sipped the amber fluid and ran through the events of the night in his mind.

He stuck by the fact that he would have waited for the police to come as Maggie had asked him. It was the gunshots that had changed his decision. He had not intentionally gone against Maggie's wishes. He really wanted her to believe that.

Joe had to concede, however, that when he followed the gunshots, his adrenaline was fired up and he liked the feel of the hunt. He wondered if this was just the way it was. Policing was in his DNA. No matter how long you were out of it, once a copper always a copper, he supposed.

He was also astute to know that he was no longer paid to police, so it had been a purely selfish motive which sent him into the cave and potential danger.

He loved Maggie and he knew that she loved him, but she fell in love with Joe Regan, antiques dealer, not DCI Joe Regan of the Met.

They had found each other late in life and, with that, both had found extreme happiness that neither thought they would ever have again. Joe now realised how his actions earlier could have jeopardised this.

He now thought of the crosses. As a boy, he could remember his grandfather telling him the story of St. Columba and his adventures. He had also told him the legend of the sacred chalice and the 12 Celtic crosses.

The story had fascinated a young Joe Regan and also fired his imagination. All these years later, to discover that they were real and to have seen them with his own eyes was unbelievable. It had been quite a night, all and all.

Joe drained his whiskey glass and pondered a refill, but decided against it. He wandered to the backdoor, opened it and stepped out into the fresh night air.

Suddenly, he heard the hoot of an owl. He always thought of the sound as comforting. Joe could recall many a night as a young boy listening to the owls while he lay in bed on his uncle and aunt's farm when he visited them in the summer holidays.

The owl sounded again. It had been a constant companion since they lived in the cottage.

Joe followed the noise. It seemed to be coming from the barn. It must be a barn owl, he thought. He had never seen one before. This might be his only chance.

Grabbing a torch from the top drawer of the pine dresser, Joe walked quietly towards the barn. When he reached the door, he slowly lifted the latch, trying not to make any noise that would frighten the bird away.

Once in the barn, he closed up the door again and shone his torch beam up into the rafters and eaves, looking for the owl. Joe saw no evidence of one, but he was shocked and startled to see a big man coming down the ladder from the loft carrying a holdall.

As the man reached the bottom of the ladder and turned around, he spotted Joe. He was as surprised to see Joe as he was him.

"What the hell are you doing here? This is private property. What the fuck are you up to?" asked Joe.

The man slowly walked forward and, in the moonlight filtering in through the timber slats of the barn, Joe recognised him as the man who was looking at the cottage the other day.

"A bit late for a trip down memory lane, isn't it?" said Joe.

The big man's face remained impassive. He then spoke.

"This bag is mine and it's not your concern. Just let me walk out of here and no harm will come to you."

"What's in the bag?" asked Joe.

Joe immediately suspected the drugs stash that the police had been combing the area for.

"None of your business and if you push me, then I'll have no choice but to hurt you. Now, just let me walk."

Joe mulled this all over. Was it really his concern? He only rented the cottage. He would be gone in a day or so. It was no skin off his nose what this man was up to, yet...

Joe heard a sudden noise behind him as the barn door opened and Maggie entered, carrying a camping lantern for light.

"Joe, I woke up suddenly and you weren't in bed. I couldn't find you. What..."

Her words froze as she saw the stranger stood in the barn.

She looked to Joe.

"What's going on? Who the hell is this?"

"I was just asking him the same question," replied Joe.

Jerry Dooley was now in a bit of a panic. He had arrived at the cottage about an hour ago. The lights were all out and the 4x4 was in the drive. He presumed that the occupiers were asleep in bed.

It was then a straightforward job to get into the barn and retrieve the drugs, get back in his van and do the drop. Sweet. But now he faced a problem with these two.

"I'm asking you both to move out the way and let me pass."

"What's in the bag?" asked Joe once again.

Jerry smiled grimly.

"You said you were an ex-copper. Still an inquisitive bastard, it seems."

Maggie suddenly spoke up.

"Tell us or you're going nowhere."

As she said this, she closed the barn door.

Jerry then let out a laugh.

"Okay. The bag is full of drugs, and it belongs to a bad man. If he doesn't get this bag within the hour, he is going to come looking for it and he doesn't care what he does to get it."

"Are these the missing drugs that the Garda are looking for?" asked Joe.

"Aye, it is," said Dooley.

"And they've been hidden in this barn all the time?"

Dooley shook his head.

"Not all the time. I had to find a new home for them quick. I originally buried them up at the abbey. I was telling the truth when I said I knew the past owner of the cottage. I knew the layout well. It seemed the perfect place to stash them and it was until you came in."

Joe called to Maggie.

"Go and phone the police now."

Maggie knew that Joe was not going to let this man go with the drugs and she understood why. Joe had a strong moral code of ethics that he could not just throw away in five minutes. These ethics had been part of him forever.

She understood this, but it did not stop her being afraid for his life every time that he took it upon himself to play sheriff. But in this day and age, how many good guys were there left? How many crusaders were willing to battle evil and put it all on the line?

"I have my mobile on me, Joe. I'm going nowhere. I'll ring them now."

"No!" bellowed Dooley.

He dropped the bag and pulled a knife from his pocket.

For the second time within a few hours, Joe faced a wicked looking blade.

"You give me no choice," snarled Dooley and slashed the blade at Joe.

Joe blocked the knife arm and drove the heel of his palm up under Dooley's nose. Anybody else receiving that blow probably would have hit the ground, but Dooley just staggered back with blood spurting from his broken nose.

Joe followed up with an intended kick to the groin, but his foot caught the inside of the big man's thigh.

Dooley now raised the blade above his head in an ice pick grip and ran forward again. This time, Joe got it right and stomped his boot into Dooley's right knee. The man howled in pain and stopped in his tracks.

Joe moved in and clapped his open palms over both of Dooley's ears and then followed that with a straight right cross to his chin. This time, Dooley did go down.

"Quick, Maggie. Grab the bag and we'll get out and lock him in here until the police comes," instructed Joe.

Maggie reacted instantly and picked up the bag. Both her and Joe ran for the door. They got outside and slid the bolt across.

Maggie punched 999 into her phone.

Joe unzipped the bag and looked at the stash of cocaine. This had a street value of hundreds of thousands.

He heard Maggie speaking to the police.

Suddenly, the doors burst open in a shower of splintering wood. Dooley had thrown his considerable weight against the rotten timbers. They were no contest for his strength. He stood with his face a mass of blood and surveyed his surroundings.

"Give me the fucking bag!" he screamed as he ran forward, blade still in hand.

Just then, a blur of ghostly white exited the barn and caught in Dooley's hair. It was the barn owl, no doubt spooked by all the noise. Dooley reached up and clutched at the bird.

Joe saw his chance. He looked at the axe in the wood chopping block behind Maggie.

"Maggie, get me the axe. Quick!"

Maggie ran and picked it up. She threw it to Joe who caught it, just as the owl flew off into the night sky.

Joe turned to see Dooley bearing down on him, knife clutched now in both hands and raised above his head ready to drive it into Joe's skull.

Joe moved to the side and brought the axe horizontally across Dooley and down, sinking the bladed edge into his right thigh.

The big man stopped instantly and howled in pain, surprised. He dropped to his knees and Joe saw the opportunity to swing the axe again, but this time, flat edge into the big man's jaw, knocking him unconscious.

Maggie ran to Joe and flung herself into his arms. Tears flooded down her face.

Joe cradled her head and whispered.

"It's okay. It's all over."

They both went back into the barn to find something to tie Dooley up with.

In the distance, they could hear police sirens getting closer.

Chapter 21

The Ink Man, aka Noel Best, pressed his phone to his ear for the umpteenth time, waiting for Jerry Dooley to answer.

The man was late for the rendezvous with him, and the four men sat in the Range Rover on the Ballykin road. These were not men who you kept waiting. Noel Best smiled nervously as he pocketed his phone.

"I'm sure he'll be here soon. It's not like him. He's always reliable."

The four men in the car said nothing, but stared balefully at him.

Dooley was already half an hour late and not answering his phone. Best was worried. *What was taking him so long?*

Then, a thought flashed through his mind. *Had Dooley double-crossed him and made off with the drugs himself?*

No. He knew whoever Best was selling them to was big. He would never get away with it. He would be hunted down like a dog.

Best looked up and down the road. It was empty. He rang again, but with no reply.

When he turned back to the Range Rover, one of men had got out. He was a big unit. Clean shaven with a flat top haircut. He was dressed in an immaculate black suit. In a thick Northern Irish accent, he spoke.

"It looks like your friend has fucked you and us both over and stolen our drugs."

Best shook his head.

"No, he'll be here. Let me ring him one more time."

With shaking hands, Best pressed Dooley's number.

It went to voicemail.

Best spoke.

"For fuck's sake, Jerry. Call me. This is urgent. What's going on?"

Best pocketed the phone and turned back to the man.

The bullet hit him straight between the eyes. He was dead before he hit the tarmac.

The big man walked forward and put two more bullets in his chest. He got back into the Range Rover and pulled out his phone as it pulled away. He looked at the others.

"Should have never trusted a fucking southerner. I better break the bad news to Mr Nolan. He isn't going to be happy."

DCI Keith Ryder stood in the entrance to the barn, watching the huge bulk of Jerry Dooley on a stretcher being transported off to hospital. A squad car followed close behind. The man was going to live, but have a hell of a headache and be walking on crutches for a while.

DCI Bryan Box, who was the lead officer on the drugs case, had been contacted and was on his way from Dublin now.

Ryder regarded Joe and Maggie.

"Well, to say you two have had an eventful day is a bit of an understatement, isn't it?"

Joe smiled wryly.

"You could say that."

"Fancy the drugs being here under ours noses all the time, the cheeky bastard," commented Ryder.

"Who is that guy? Do you know?" asked Maggie.

Ryder pulled out his notebook.

"He is Jerry Aidan Dooley. A known associate of Noel Best, aka The Ink Man. Best is known to us for peddling drugs and has a few convictions. He owns a tattoo parlour in Cork and uses it as a front for his dodgy dealings. He is very much a middleman for somebody bigger who we are yet to discover. We had him down as the number one suspect to receive this shipment of cocaine, but when we searched his premises and his flat, it was clean. It threw us out for sure, but maybe we underestimated the slippery bastard. He was one step ahead of us. Anyway, we'll now be visiting Mr Best very soon to see what he has got to say for himself."

Joe regarded the disappearing ambulance.

"A few days back, this Dooley character was here taking a look at the cottage. I guess he was checking the place out. He said he used to know the owner and did work for him. Anyway, to get to the point, I had seen him up at the dig at the abbey so say helping out. I suspect maybe the dig site might have been the first place he thought to bury the drugs, but something must have gone wrong. Do you think there's any connection to him and this Leary guy and the crosses?"

Ryder stroked his chin thoughtfully.

"Maybe. It's too early to say. We won't really know until this Dermot Leary and Dooley recover consciousness and start talking."

"I'm going to put the kettle on. Would you like a drink?" said Maggie.

DCI Ryder smiled.

"A black coffee, two sugars would seem in order. Thanks."

Maggie went into the cottage and Joe followed her. In the kitchen, he took her hand and looked deeply into her eyes.

"Maggie, are we alright? I swear I don't want to hurt you and I certainly don't want to lose you. I know I can be hot-headed sometimes and impulsive. Too many years in the job has conditioned me that way. I realise I have to change my ways for both of our sakes, but I need you to help me. Can you forgive me and let me try again?"

Maggie looked up at Joe. Tears were forming in her eyes, but he also saw a steely resolve there.

"Joe, I can't pretend that I understand all you went through in the force or the horrors you witnessed. I do know you have a strong sense of right and wrong and you find it hard to walk away from situations, but after the Brendan Quinn incident where we both could have lost our lives, you agreed to step away from things and try to live a normal life. I don't want to force you into that if you still harbour the need to keep policing, but I can't live with that Joe. Each time you start playing detective, I fear that you're not coming home to me."

Joe embraced her and Maggie slid into his arms.

"I understand, Maggie. This series of events, I truly didn't go looking for. It just happened. Wrong place, wrong time. I can't pretend I didn't get that thrill of the chase again, but I'm also smart enough to realise I'm not 25 anymore. What can I say? I'm an old fool."

Maggie smiled.

"Okay, Joe. Old fool, you can be now and again, but I love you and I want to be with you."

"I want to be with you too, Maggie. More than anything," replied Joe.

They kissed and held each other, both inwardly counting their blessings.

In the coming weeks, Thomas Cahill was released from hospital. He and Shannon were free of any charges and there was word that they may receive some reward money from the finding of the crosses as the chalice was found on the dig site of the abbey which they were in charge of. They hoped that the reward would be enough for that trip to the States.

No suspicion was cast upon either of them. If Leary recovered consciousness, it would be his word against theirs as to what happened and the evidence against Leary did not look good.

Two bodies had washed up by the old lighthouse. The lighthouse keeper who checked monthly on the beacon light found them both one morning washed in onto the rocks. They had been in the sea a while and were badly decomposed. Every little nibbler in the sea had had a go at them, but they appeared to be two men in their late twenties. There was no form of identity on either of them.

Forensics showed that they had not died from drowning, but by blunt force trauma to the head. What was of interest to the Garda was the discovery inside the zipped jacket pocket of one of them a gold lighter engraved, *To my dearest Declan, Love Mary*. This opened up new possibilities in the murder case of the professor.

The body of Andrew Sharkey has not yet been found.

Dermot Leary finally awoke, but maintained that he had no memory whatsoever of any of the events outlined to him. Further in-depth medical tests needed to be performed on him. Doctors have said that he may never remember exactly what happened. The Garda are waiting to see the outcome.

The bag of drugs was impounded and the powers to be extremely pleased with how things panned out.

Jerry Dooley recovered consciousness and is now in police custody waiting to be charged.

Joe is in line for a bravery award, as is Bertie Neal.

The body of Noel Best was found on the coast road by a dog walker. The Garda have no leads as to what happened to him at this moment in time.

The British Museum is in contact with the owners of the Clover Leaf Golf Club, Hotel and Spa about the purchase of the chalice and crosses for permanent display at their prestigious premises. Clover Leaf stand to make a lot of money.

Bertie Neal has become a bit of a local celebrity due to his involvement in the whole episode. He is down for appearances on BBC and ITV news programmes. He is looking forward to his ITV appearance, especially meeting presenter Susanna Reid. He wondered if she was in a relationship at present. Well, a man has got to try.

Joe and Maggie finally left Ballykin after giving their evidence and headed to Cork for the final leg of their holiday. While visiting the romantic Blarney Castle, Joe proposed to Maggie, and she accepted. A spring wedding was on the cards next year and a honeymoon in Hawaii.

Epilogue

The man pressed speed dial on his phone and waited. As soon as it was connected, he spoke.

"It's me. I haven't much time. I'm on my way into a meeting. I'm contacting you for an update on the situation."

The voice on the other end answered.

"Ah, Mr Ryan. I was expecting you sooner. The situation is as follows. Your bag of cocaine is at present under lock and key at Carrickburn Police Station. It's going to be moved to Dublin in a day or so. It will be destroyed by the forensic science laboratory."

Ryan cut in.

"I can't allow that to happen. I expect you to substitute that bag before it leaves and then we'll arrange a meet for you to give it to my men. Is that understood, Detective Chief Inspector?"

"Okay. I'm on it."

There was a pause and then Ryan spoke again.

"This man, Jerry Dooley, is he likely to start squealing to get a lighter sentence?"

"I doubt it, Mr Ryan. He knew nothing beyond Noel Best. He's not a danger."

"What about this ex-copper, Regan?"

"Same. He's no threat. He'll be heading back home in a few days."

"And we know where home is, do we?" queried Ryan.

"We do. Yes. As I said, he's out of the picture and not a concern."

Ryan mulled this over, then asked.

"And Best?"

"No witnesses and no forensics. Best was a lowlife. The Garda won't be busting a gut to hunt down his killer."

"I'll take your word for all this. I hope you won't let me down. Things got a little messy here. We can't afford that to happen again," said Ryan.

"I agree, Mr Ryan. We'll have to be more careful next time. It was just an unfortunate set of circumstances."

"Indeed, DCI Box. Particularly unfortunate for me. It's extra pressure I do not need, so sort this matter out for me."

The phone disconnected and DCI Bryan Box slipped it in his inside pocket.

He picked up his takeaway coffee cup from the table and left McDonalds. He did not want to be in the habit of pissing off James Noah Ryan. He was a powerful businessman and a regular benefactor to the Northern Ireland parliament.

The man had strong political ambitions himself. His generous donations were always greatly received from parliament. They were not aware, of course, that they came from illegal drug deals.

James Ryan was a valuable asset and would be instrumental in the coming elections. His money would be gratefully received, but no doubt he would want something in exchange when the time came...

Other Books by the Author

If you enjoyed this book, then check out
other stories by Kevin.
Read a little about them on the following pages.
Available at Amazon, Waterstones
and all good bookstores.

For more information, visit www.kevinohagan.com
or join the group "Kevin O'Hagan
Author's Corner" on Facebook.

Battlescars

Tony Slade Novel number 1

Some wounds run deep. Can they ever heal?

Tony Slade sits in a coffee shop waiting. He is reflecting on his dark and violent past. He is waiting for the woman he loves, but he is also waiting for the man who wants him dead. Who will reach him first? The clock is ticking...

Tony Slade is used to dealing with violence and death. He has made a career out of it. From boxer to bouncer, paratrooper, and mercenary to minder. But now, he is getting older, and he wants out. He has miraculously found love and he has one last chance at happiness, but it will come with a price. The woman he loves is not his; she belongs to a very dangerous man. A man who you do not want to cross. But Tony is ready to risk it all on one last roll of the dice before a powder keg of violence explodes.

But that is not all. Unknown to him, there is another threat coming his way. One that he will not see until the last moment. Who will get out alive?

Tough times call for tough people. Tony Slade is one such person.

No Hiding Place

Tony Slade Novel number 2

You can run, but you can't hide forever.

They say time is a great healer. But for Tony Slade time is running out. The physical scars are healing, but the mental ones are still raw. Waking up in hospital after the coffee shop massacre and finding he has cheated death; he needs to know why. But he has now become a man everybody wants to question. All he wants to do is disappear forever, but some people will not let that happen.

Suddenly, Tony is hounded by the press and media. He is also trailed by the tenacious DCI Wyatt and hunted by a psychotic killer who is relentless and hell bent on revenge.

Tony Slade is in hiding, recovering from the bullet wounds and the trauma of recent events that have changed his life forever. Hiding on the tiny, isolated island of *Graig O Mor* in the Bristol Channel, Tony knows that it is only a matter of time until he is found. Then, he will have to stop running and make a stand against an enemy who will not give up. It will become a matter of life and death.

*A storm is coming from the mainland
to the Island of Graig O Mor.*

Last Stand

Tony Slade Novel number 3

Blood is thicker than water.

Tony Slade is living in the Canary Islands. He is resting and soaking up the sun. He is keeping his head down under an assumed identity and trying to forget the last few traumatic years where he has experienced love, violence, heartbreak and death.

Tony is a survivor. An ex-paratrooper and mercenary who has seen more than his fair share of action, but those days are well behind him now. Or so he thought.

He is no longer a young man and the fire that used to burn like an inferno in his belly is now just flickering. Tony is looking for a quiet life into retirement when he receives a shocking and lifechanging piece of news. A secret that has been buried for years has suddenly came to light.

This secret will force Tony out of hiding to return to the UK and back into the violent world of gangsters, drugs and crime.

Pursued all the time by an old nemesis, Tony must pull all his fighting skills together to face a dangerous and deadly drug lord who has something of his that he wants back at any cost. Tony knows that blood will spill in one final stand.

This time, it's personal.

Killing Time

Ex-Scotland Yard policeman DCI Joe Regan had retired from the force after a particularly vicious attempt on his life, which had him on the critical list in hospital, but his gritty Gaelic spirit and resolve helped him recover.

Now leading a new life running an antiques emporium in the sleepy town of Oakcombe in the West Country, he is trying to put his past behind him. But unknown to Joe, a burglary at the nearby country home of famous TV celebrity Ron Goodwin opens up a nasty can of worms in the form of something hidden within an antique clock which finds its way to his shop.

This something could ruin Ron Goodwin's career just as he is about to crack America. The dark secrets contained within the clock cannot afford to fall into the wrong hands, so it must be found at all costs, even if it means murder.

Joe Regan suddenly finds himself embroiled in a race to find the clock and its contents as they go missing, before a hired killer who will stop at nothing does. But when Joe inadvertently stumbles across the secret, he now becomes the next target.

The clock is ticking, and time is running out.

A Change of Heart

*Can a heart transplant victim inherit
the characteristics of their donor?*

Simon Winter is a prime candidate for a heart attack. Middle aged, sedentary and grossly overweight. His lifestyle is driving him to an early grave, but he is ignoring all the signs until it is too late.

He has a failed marriage behind him, a boring job and a fear of violence and blood. He has lived a safe and uneventful life, avoiding confrontation and danger until now where this is all about to change dramatically.

Eddie Prince is an ex-professional boxer and minor television celebrity. He has had a turbulent life out of the ring, which has resulted in prison time. Money has come and gone as he has a gambling addiction, which results in him owing a lot of money to some bad people. He has run away to what he hopes is a better life, but his old life is about to catch up with him, resulting in dire circumstances.

These two men are about to connect in a way they could never have dreamed of. Two men at different ends of the spectrum. Two men who are chalk and cheese. Two men who have nothing in common until one inherits the other's heart after a transplant.

Now, one will use the other as a vessel of revenge to find the man who murdered him and settle a score with shocking conclusions.

Blood Tracks

At one time in the 1980s, Stormtrooper were the most successful rock band on the planet. Everything they touched turned to gold. But among all the fame was jealousy and greed. This resulted in the sacking of their iconic lead singer Jimmy Parrish for drug usage, which endangered the band's continued success.

Sometime later after a bitter break-up, Jimmy Parrish apparently committed suicide in mysterious circumstances. His body was never found. A proposed warts and all book on the band that he had been approached to write would now never happen, a blessing for some.

The Mark 2 line-up of the band went on to have global success and entered the Rock and Roll Hall of Fame as one of the biggest rock bands of all time. Even when they finally split up, the spectre of Jimmy Parrish never fully went away.

Fast forward twenty years, the band have reformed to record a new album. They are heading for the remote island of Ruma off the Outer Hebrides. Ruma is a wild isolated place of mystery and intrigue. They will stay at the grand house of a reclusive film director who has a state-of-the-art recording studio in the bowels of the building.

Storm Alec is due to hit the island. It will cut it and its inhabitants off from the rest of civilisation.

But worse is to come as a mysterious killer lurks within the walls of the house hellbent on murdering each and every member of the band and their recording crew.

Who is it and what is their motive?

There is nowhere to run and nowhere to hide. Nobody is coming to help.

As the body count rises, who - if anybody - can survive.

Making a hit record can sometimes be murder.

The Key to Murder

Is money the root of all evil?

Imagine that you found a key. A key that opened a locker. A locker that contained a holdall. A holdall that contained money. A lot of money. £350,000, to be exact, in used untraceable notes.

What would you do?

Put it back in the locker and walk away? Contact the police? Or take it?

It is a lifechanging sum.

But what if that money belonged to a dangerous man? A man who will stop at nothing to get it back. He will relentlessly track you down and anybody who gets in his way will suffer.

This is what happens when the worlds of three men clash.

Ronnie Moon, Tommy Scott and Adam Lucas are all involved in a deadly game of Cat and Mouse. Each want the money for different reasons.

The hunt is on, but who will survive?

Their greed and ambition could just be the Key to Murder.

If you want to know what man is really like, take notice of what he is really like when he loses money.

Murder in Store

"You know what they say about curiosity, don't you?"

Chris Cooper is nicknamed the 'Nighthawk'. He and his friends are urban explorers. They love to enter abandoned buildings and structures and search them, especially at night when nobody else is around. The activity is illegal, but it gives them such a buzz that it becomes addictive. They love to flirt with danger.

Eddie Creed is on the run to Bristol. He has inadvertently crossed 'Big Baz' Watkins, a London criminal with a nasty reputation. Eddie only wanted to help the girl, but now his world is turned upside down as three hitmen are on his trail. Their agenda is to kill him.

On this particular cold winter's evening, Chris and his friends will enter and explore the empty store of the iconic Radley's in Bristol city centre.

On this same night, Eddie Creed, who is being chased down by the hitmen, seeks refuge and finds it in the same store. When the killers also enter the store and block off its only exit, a shocking and horrifying series of events begins to unfold.

Suddenly, the worlds of Eddie Creed and Chris Cooper and his friends collide as mayhem and murder occurs. Now, they are all running for their lives as they are relentlessly hunted down.

There will be murder in store!

About the Author

Kevin O'Hagan lives just outside Bristol with his wife. He has three grown-up children and five grandchildren.

Kevin has had a passion for writing since he was a child but has no formal writing training. Everything he has learnt has been a personal voyage of discovery.

One of his favourite sayings is, "If you want to get better at writing, then write."

Buried Secrets is his 9th work of fiction to date.

Kevin is a semi-retired world-renowned martial artist. He holds an 8th Dan black belt in Jujutsu after more than 48 years of training and teaching. These days, he still teaches part-time.

His hobbies are reading, writing, playing guitar, going to the gym and travelling.

www.kevinohagan.com for more information.